# INTRODUCTION
## ALIZE

**FIFTEEN YEARS AGO: 2008**

"Shawty, I'm tired of taking shorts behind yo' dirty ass! You either slide me some more fuckin' money, or you gon' earn the rest some kind of way. Bitch don't ever come with nothing but bullshit and excuses. Always coming 'round here trying to finesse a nigga. Ain't shit in this motherfuckin' world free, Niecy," the coal-black young boy argued in his heavy southern drawl.

The young man I spoke of went by the name of Black, and he was obviously fed up with my mother Niecy since he was going off on her, face twisted into a scowl, volume level on ten. In return, my mother stood there silently, looking shameful. With his beady eyes fixed hard on her, he waited for a reply.

My own young eyes filled with sadness as I observed her standing there stumbling over her words, doing her best to come up with an adequate response after his truthful insults. I hated when my mother begged, but even more, I hated when she was disappointed. She'd just stolen a couple packs of steaks out of Kroger to scrounge up that eight dollars that she'd just tried to hand to Black. She'd been so excited when she made it out the store without being detected by security guards, and even more excited when she secured a quick sale for the meat to a guy named Benny who she claimed was a good friend of hers, although he sure didn't act like one. She'd only wanted twenty dollars for it, but of course her "friend" Benny talked her down, shoving a crumpled ten-dollar bill in her hand as payment. She was instructed to 'take it or leave it.' Needless to say, she took it. In her opinion, something was better than nothing. Despite being shorted, she was still in good spirits when she and I headed over to the alleyway that we were standing in so she could buy a bag of crack.

She was only two dollars short and it was for good reason. She'd just taken two of that ten to buy my dinner; a bag of Chee-tos, a swiss roll and a can of grape soda. It was my favorite combination of snacks, and after running around in the sun for hours, I devoured it in a few minutes. I almost felt at fault for Black's tirade. I couldn't help but wish that I never mentioned my rumbling stomach. If I hadn't, she would've had enough for the bag of poison that she'd come for.

Even though drugs weren't good for her, I wanted her to have them so she would be happy. I hated so much to see her saddened. Face full of sorrow and defeat. Even more, I hated how her disappointment was going to affect me. The sky was pitch black, and after running the streets all day and night with her, my eleven-year-old body was exhausted. However, I knew if she didn't get her final hit for the night, then sleep would prob-ably never come for either of us. And sleep was something I desperately needed. I hadn't been feeling well the past day or so. I had a headache, was weak, and for some reason, my legs and arms were sore. Like I'd run a race. Despite all that, I didn't bother complaining. I didn't want my mom in a bad mood, arguing at me about slowing her down.

"Come on, Black. You can let me slide for two?" My mother begged. Her eyes were buck while her dry lips trembled in antic-ipation of her next hit. "You know I'm good for it. My money always been good with you, but this time I had to buy my daughter something to eat."

She glanced down at me, doing her best to conjure up some sort of sympathy from Black.

"I don't give a fuck!" he snapped, causing her to jump. "You always short, and I know damn well yo' ass get food stamps so I ain't tryin' to hear them lame ass excuses, shawty. And you know I don't usually sell nothing less than twenties," he boasted like that was top tier. Even though I hadn't been on earth long, I still knew that wasn't much in the drug world.

"Either go find some more money or figure out a way to make up the rest," he told her. He stared at her while everyone in the alley snickered. "The question is ... what are you willing to do for this here?"

His anger seemed to have subsided, and he was now taunting her. Black reached in his pocket and pulled out a small plastic baggie containing individually wrapped pieces of drugs. He then began to tease her by wagging it back and forth in her face, causing her to nearly salivate.

My eyes lowered to the ground from the embarrassment of what he was implying. I was young, but I was well before my time. I knew exactly what he was suggesting. I knew my mother did some strange things for drugs. I'd witnessed it on more than one occasion. I'd seen her on her knees servicing people when my eyes were supposed to be closed or I was supposed to have my back turned, looking away. I'd watched her rob other prostitutes as well as other addicts. Tell them she would go grab drugs for them and never return. I'd also seen her offer to run to the store for neighbors or dope boys, but she'd never go. Instead, she'd just keep the money – ducking and dodging them until they eventually caught up with her and beat her bloody over a few dollars. Black knew full-well there wasn't much that she *wouldn't* do for those drugs. Eyes still lowered, I eventually dropped my entire head and focused on the grime coated pavement lining the alley. I was one of those kids that didn't say much. I was quiet. Only speaking when spoken to.

"What you want me to do?" she asked with desperation in her voice.

I didn't remember how it happened or when it happened, but drugs had gotten a firm grip on my mother's soul. She seemed to no longer have any self-respect or any pride. What started off as a secret addiction, eventually became full-blown and consuming. From the moment we woke up, until the time we went to sleep, all she thought about was getting more drugs.

"Whatchu trying to do?" he asked.

"Dis nigga, boy. You stay doing weird, nasty shit," one of the younger boys called out in disgust.

My eyes shifted to the familiar voice. They landed on another dark-skinned guy with short starter locs in his head. His name was Lance. He was younger than the other men he hung around and only a few years older than me. Everyone paused for a second, looked at my mom and then simultaneously burst into laughter before Black finally answered.

"I don't know what you got yo' lips all puckered up for bitch. I damn sure ain't 'bout to let you put those crusty ass mafucka's on me," he cackled before more laughter erupted through the alley. "Fuck that. You better find something else more appropriate. This bitch geekin," he continued to laugh before turning his attention back to Lance. His faced hardened some.

"And nigga stop complaining about how we treat smokers 'round here. If you don't like how I do shit, where *I run shit*, roll," he said evenly. "I know how you got a soft spot for them and all," he continued, following up with a quiet chuckle.

Lance didn't respond. He just stood there and matched Black's cold gaze for a moment before mumbling something and looking away.

"Yo, I be right back," someone said aloud, ending their tense stare down.

"Where you going?" Black asked, turning towards the guy that just spoke.

"Down some. I gotta take a piss."

The alley we were standing in was right alongside of a run-down, crime-infested apartment complex. It started at the front of the complex and led to the next street

I looked over at the boy who was speaking. It was another young boy named Cj. He was a light-skinned guy. Frail with two raggedy cornrows going straight down the back of his head. I'd seen him around plenty of times since my mother usually brought drugs from the same area. He couldn't have been no more than fifteen or sixteen years old. He started to walk off and head towards the back, but Black stopped him.

"Na. You good. You ain't gotta do that. I know exactly how we can put this crack-hoe to use. I gotcha toilet bowl right here," he snickered.

"Nigga you nasty as fuck." He laughed, shrugging him off even though his face looked like he was seriously contemplating it.

"I'm dead ass. It's pissy enough around this mafucka as it is. If she wants this ooowee, she 'gon catch that pee-pee." Black held the bag back up and laughed some more.

"Well shit, I might as well get my dick sucked for all of that then. Mouth already gon' be open. Plus, I heard she had that lockjaw."

"Enter at yo' own risk nigga," Black advised. "I wouldn't let that bitch crusty ass mouth touch me," he said as his face wrinkled in disgust.

Even though I loved my mom, I couldn't blame him. Once a caramel-colored beauty, she was now skinny and dirty with a few teeth missing from the front.

"Shit ... I can't catch shit from a little neck," Cj replied.

"If that's what you want, then that's what you get." Black shrugged before motioning for my mother to follow Cj.

"Go on and serve my patna if you want this work for that lil eight-dollars you got," he said to my mom, before turning his attention back to CJ. "And make sure you piss in that hoe mouth and not in this fuckin' alley nigga. Do that shit right over there for niggas to see. I want to set an example. Let mafucka's know that they can't keep coming 'round this bitch short. We stripping mafucka's of they dignity 'round this bitch."

"Oh, don't worry." He chuckled before reaching down and rubbing his crotch. "She gon' get this piss *and* this cum. Come on!" Cj barked.

I lowered my head back to the ground in a shame that I had no business knowing anything about. I knew what all their words meant, and I knew the power dudes like that held in the neighborhood because of the drugs they slung. I prayed my mother pulled me in the direction that we'd came in. I prayed that she'd forget all about the drugs she'd came for. Unfortunately, God didn't hear me. Like the true, tired fiend she was, my mother let go of my hand and mumbled, "Alize, go stand on the street and wait for me."

I didn't reply. A light wave of dizziness and nausea rushed over me, but I quickly shook it off. I took a few deep breaths and blinked a couple times before holding my head back up and mumbling 'okay'.

"Come on nigga, you ain't gotta do that shit. You geekin'. Her daughter with her knowing what you 'bout to have her mama doing for folks to see. Just let her slide. All that other shit is unnecessary," I heard Lance say before wagging his head and frowning.

"Nigga fuck her!" Black countered sharply, dismissing Lance's last plea for fairness.

"Drink up bitch," I heard another man laugh before I turned my back and took off out the alley.

About fifteen-minutes later, my mother emerged from the alley and showed up on the street where I had been patiently waiting for her return. Her eyes were red, her nose was running, and her nappy hair was wet and had been pushed back as if she'd tried to make it look presentable before facing me. She adjusted her twisted blouse that was also wet, wiped her hand on her pants, and then quietly took my hand. Her eyes darted around, and I could tell she was anxious to get away from the complex. I expected to see shame in her face but surprisingly, I saw none at all.

"You ready to go?" she asked, before slipping her hand into mine and speed-walking back to the abandoned house a few blocks away that we'd been staying at for the past few months. She'd always told me that it was just temporary. That one day we would have our own place.

Although people saw us there on a regular basis, namely other addicts, I'd been sternly instructed not to tell anyone that we'd been staying there. Not the staff where I sporadically attended school and most importantly, not my aunt Melva, my mother's sister. She was judgmental and dramatic, according to my mother.

My aunt Melva had tried to intervene several times in reference to my care. It never worked since anytime Aunt Melva offered to take me in, my mother would tell her that I was just fine with her and then disappear to keep her 'hypocritical, money-hungry ass out' of her business. Her words, not mine.

My mother's latest disappearance to avoid Aunt Melva had landed us in another crime-ridden section of Atlanta called Lakewood Heights, residing in a rodent infested, dilapidated home. At one point, the home may had been considered nice; now it was dirty, the sides were peeling, and the house itself was covered with vines and surrounded with untamed bushes and vegetation. Most of the windows were boarded up while others had their boards snatched off and windows shattered, likely to gain entrance.

"Mom, I'm tired," I whined a few minutes after we settled in our section of the dark, musty basement we illegally occupied. Although no one slept in the main quarters of the bando, it was discreetly, but heavily trafficked by hookers and dealers during the day and night. The cops patrolled the streets, but they didn't have the manpower to control who went in and out of the countless abandoned homes that littered the city.

"Is it okay for me to lay down?" I asked, my eyes heavy with fatigue.

Even though my mom was a crackhead, she kept me pasted to her side night and day, unlike other chicks with the same addiction. Their kids usually roamed the streets freely. I had only asked to lay down because if my mom wasn't done running around, then there was no point of torturing myself. I loved a good sleep, and I hated being woken early from one. It didn't matter if it was three in the morning, if my mom hit the pavement, then I was going to be right with her. She would never leave me in a bando by myself. Even though I was eleven, I didn't look much older than eight or nine. I was malnourished because I was constantly on the go and hardly ever ate a home-cooked meal. Chips, cakes, and sodas mostly made up my diet. I was lucky to have any of my teeth. At least that's what Aunt Melva told me whenever I saw her.

"Yeah, go ahead," she said, her back turned to me in the corner where she was quickly preparing her drugs.

I walked a few feet away to a corner where I had a thin tattered Tweety Bird blanket and pillow that formed my makeshift bed. I took a seat and pulled off my smelly, dirty K-Swiss. I laid down, pulled my blanket to my chin and closed my eyes. A few minutes later, my head was still pounding and despite my assumptions, laying down actually made it worse. I nuzzled my head into the dingy, but cool pillow in an attempt to soothe it. While I moved around with my eyes closed, I heard the flick of a lighter and a few seconds later, the sound of my mother inhaling deeply. I knew she was smoking the rocks that she'd just gotten from Black.

After laying down for a few minutes, sharp pains circulated through my stomach and it began to churn violently. I sat up. I knew I was about to hurl. Before I could warn my mother that I was about to be sick, I threw up all over my blanket, pillow and self. Thick vomit mostly orange and brown in color ran down my shirt.

"Alize! What the fuck!" my mother spun around and yelled while I sat teary-eyed and shaking. "Why didn't you try to get that nasty shit into something?" she asked, her eyes now extremely buggy from the Cocaine high that she was experiencing.

I wasn't physically ready to respond. Still heaving, I sniffled and spit out a few specks of vomit.

"Fuck! That shit gon' have it stinking as a motherfucker down here. It's already fucked up down here," she argued with little sympathy.

"Mommy, I don't feel good," I moaned, clutching my stomach as more sharp pains began to pass through it.

My mother finally stood up from the corner she was in and walked over to me, using the back of her rough hand to feel my forehead.

"Shit! You're burning up," she said, her eyes bulging out even further then they previously were.

Another round of dizziness washed over me. That time I wasn't able to shake it off like I'd done earlier in the lobby. Everything in front of me seemed to be blurry and spinning.

"Mom—" I attempted to speak but my eyes began to get heavy, and I became enclosed in darkness.

I woke up a few hours later at Southside Medical Center. I only knew because of a large sign on the wall bearing its name. A large clock nearby advised me that it was three in the morning, in bold black letters. I hadn't been there too long. I was in a cold room with a needle taped to my arm and attached to a plastic bag holding fluid. My eyes were parted partially but I saw my mother, hair standing on top of her hair looking defensive. She was talking to a white lady in a uniform that appeared to be a nurse. A police officer stood by the door and looked on but said nothing.

"She has Rat Bite Fever."

"Rat Bite what?" my mother asked, her arms wrapped around her upper body like she was cold.

"Rat Bite Fever. It's a disease caused by bacteria transmitted from rodents. Usually from bites or consumption of food or water contaminated with the urine and droppings of rodents carrying the bacteria. Has your daughter mentioned being bit by anything? Or have you seen any rats in your home?" the nurse asked.

My mother shook her head. She was lying. The bando that we stayed in had rodents crawling all through it.

"Has she complained about feeling ill or have you noticed that she's appeared ill in the past few days? Been tired?"

"Not that I've noticed. And she hasn't complained about anything."

The nurse nodded and took a few notes on the paper attached to the clipboard she was holding.

"Did you notice the large rash on her back?" she asked, peering at my mother.

Once again, she shook her head; however, this time she lowered her eyes in shame.

"Well, she has quite a large rash on her back. That's another symptom of the disease. Considering her state: the rash, the vomiting, the fever, it's safe to say that she's probably had this a few weeks. We looked her over and saw a few old bites that were healing up."

The nurse paused for a moment. I knew she was about to give us some bad news when I saw her glance at the officer who was still standing quietly by the door.

"Now, Mom we are in no way blaming you, but unfortunately, we're not able to let her go home with you until we can evaluate and approve your living conditions. Do you have anyone – a relative maybe that is willing to take her until then?"

I watched as my mother hesitated and then finally respond. "Yeah. My sister."

"Good, because in cases like this, if you didn't have someone, then we would have to temporarily place her into state custody."

While I was able to watch, I was still too weak to respond. My mother stood there silently with her arms folded against her chest. For the past few years, she'd tried so hard to keep me out the grasp of my Aunt Melva only to still end up having to hand me over to her. I couldn't help but notice the defeat in her face. I knew what she was thinking because the same thoughts were going through my head as well. With my mother's out of control crack addiction and our living situation, there was no way that she was going to ever get me back.

## ALIZE
### PRESENT DAY

**D**read settled in the pit of my stomach as I gripped the top of the last big, black Hefty bag carrying the remainder of my belongings. Despite fighting tooth and nail to keep from being evicted, I was still found in violation of my lease agreement and was being forced from the property. Not only was I angry, I was disappointed in myself for taking the bait and letting a hoe and a bitch ass nigga jeopardize where my children laid their heads.

It had barely been a month since I'd caught my man and baby's daddy Neal and neighbor Melissa fucking in my bed after coming back home abruptly from what was supposed to be a day out with my girls. I couldn't lie, I was hurt, and it was that hurt that led me to go dumb and turn the fuck up. Disregarding the fact that I was on subsidized housing, I chose to step outside of my character and walk Melissa's ass like the dog she was. Before she could part her mouth to conjure up a lie about why she was naked in my house, I had my fist connected with it. Once I was on her ass, there wasn't much left that she could do. She was bigger than me, but she was also slower. To put it frankly, she wasn't fuckin' with me with the hands, so I was tearing her ass up all over that room while my girls looked on.

Being the hoe-saving ass nigga that he was, Neal tried to intervene; however, I was in a blind, passion-induced rage caused by betrayal from the one person I trusted. As soon as his hands touched me, I went into attack mode on him as well. I pushed my girls out the room and then dashed over and snatched up the gun that he always carried and placed on the nightstand when he laid down. As soon as I scooped it up, I cocked it just like he'd shown me countless times and proceeded to let that bitch rip on the both of them. I squeezed the trigger twice. One shot for both of them. I wasn't proud. It was a stupid move that could have landed someone dead and me in prison.

Luckily for the two of them, my aim was poor, and I wound up missing. I guess that worked out for me in the long run. Unfortunately, my luck began to run out right after. Some other nosy ass neighbor ended up calling in the sound of gun shots, but my baby's daddy Neal nor hoe ass Melissa cooperated. Had they did, my ass would have been booked in the city jail and my kids would have been in somebody's foster home. Despite the fact that I wasn't charged, the nosey bitch from the rental office came into my apartment and saw the bullet holes. Not even a month later, my kids and I were out on the streets. What pissed me off the most was the scary bitch in management found the balls to evict me but couldn't keep violence down by evicting the hoes who had the terrorizing ass niggas running in and out of their spots. Shootings, brawls, and even stabbings weren't uncommon in my complex. Still dragging our belongings, I finally reached the front door where my girls were standing.

"Come on y'all," I said so they could follow me out.

With my two children trailing behind me, I walked out the front door with my head held high on purpose. I knew as soon as I stepped foot out that door, it was going to be hoes standing out there staring in my face instead of watching they kids. They would probably be expecting to see me crying and looking ashamed. I wasn't about to give any of them the satisfaction. Despite my past and circumstances, I knew I was still better then damn near all them broke-down busted bitches. They didn't want shit and didn't have shit except an apartment and a nigga to occasionally fuck and suck on. To be honest, I was one of the badder bitches in the complex. I wasn't bragging; it was what it was. Brown-skinned with a shoulder-length bob, cute face, hooded eyes, and a curvy body, I was kinda tough. I didn't even have the big fat ass that hoes lugged around with them, but I still caused a little frenzy. As much money as Neal was allegedly getting, I shouldn't have even been living amongst that bullshit. Instead of putting up a fuss so he could move us out the hood, I fell into the same thinking pattern of those around me. I got comfortable and content with having a little extra while everyone around me watched in envy.

I was no longer the person to envy. I was the person to pity. Just like I expected, as soon as my right sneaker touched the pavement outside the door, the cock-eating hoe that was the sole reason behind my eviction was staring me right in my face with a smirk. I didn't care though. Those same lips were all the way upside down not long ago, when I beat the brakes off her ass. It was the wrong move, but it was the principal. And principal was big where I was from.

While Melissa played tough with her two homegirls beside her, attempting to antagonize me by staring all up in my face, I turned towards her and met her gaze. Only mine was more looming. After a few seconds, I tore my eyes away from her ugly mug to unlock the door of my sky-blue Hyundai Elantra so I could usher my girls into the car. Once I had them buckled in and closed the door on them, I spun back around and turned to Melissa.

"You got a problem?" I asked her.

"Nope. I ain't got no problems, but it seems like you do, considering the fact that you just got put the fuck out." She chuckled.

For a moment, I thought about running to her door, charging her, and choking her until she passed out; however, I knew them hoes weren't going to do shit but either jump me or call the police. Melissa the maggot was right about one thing; I did have a problem, and it was way more important than beating her up again.

"You see bitch, that's the difference between you and me. I don't see a problem, I see an opportunity," I lied. I was definitely scared to death about having no place to stay with my girls, but I figured I was going to talk my shit anyway.

"While yo' washed-up, funky, lumpy ass still around here suckin' dick, I'll be making shit happen. Trust and believe I won't be down for long."

"We'll see," she said, just as I turned my back on her and proceeded to hop in my car.

I didn't waste any time starting it up and peeling out the parking lot of the little raggedy ass, graffiti-laden, trash strewn neighborhood that I'd called home for the past five years. Good fuckin' riddance. I needed something different anyway. I needed to be pushed out of my comfort zone. I just hated *how* I was being pushed out of my comfort zone.

After driving for a few minutes, I pulled into a gas station that was void of annoying ass water boys to get some gas. Before I hopped out, I grabbed my phone out of my Coach bag and checked it. Just like I expected, I had three missed calls from Neal. I looked back at my girls, turned back around and sighed. As much as I despised their sorry, cheating-ass daddy, I knew I was going to have to call him back. I hated to admit it, let alone say it, but I needed him. The whole time I was with Neal, he was the breadwinner, which I had grown up thinking was the way of life. Find a man that loves you and takes care of you. I was truly ashamed that I hadn't been on my shit saving money like I should have been, especially after Neal's behavior and actions stopped matching his words.

Ever since I'd caught him fucking Melissa, I had been ignoring him. While I was fighting the eviction, he would try and pop up, but I'd threaten to call the police. He'd call but I would send him to voicemail. The one time I did try and have a civilized conversation with him about the girls, he wanted to talk about us moving past what had happened. He had me fucked up. I loved with my whole heart, but I also hated with that bitch in its entirety too.

Believe it or not, Neal and I hadn't always been at each other's throat. We were actually happy at one point. I'd been with him since I was seventeen, and for the most part, he'd always been good to me. He always worked and took care of me and our little family. We weren't rich and since rent was expensive in the A, we lived in the hood. We had our struggles, but we always made it work. It was only recently --- about two years ago, that we'd started having problems. Neal had unexpectedly lost his job at a little paper company he'd been working at since he was a teen. Being the nigga that he was, he hopped on the next grind immediately so he could continue to be the provider that he'd always been. Unfortunately, that hustle wasn't legal. Neal's cousin Boobie was a heavy weight in the city. A dope dealer that pushed a lot of product and was well known in the Oakland City neighborhood we lived and practically grew up in. It was nothing for him to put Neal on.

From the very start of Neal's illegal endeavors, Boobie hit him with enough dope to supply other street level dealers. Instead of going directly to Boobie for the weight, they were instructed to hit Neal for it. With that arrangement, Neal became a mid-level boss overnight. Putting him in position was nothing to Boobie; he actually preferred it that way. He did his best to surround himself with niggas that he could trust, and he knew he could definitely trust Neal.

Even though the money was good, the side-effects that came with it were not. Overnight Neal became a different person. Drug-dealing had hardened him. Turned him into a gun-toting thug. The hardworking family man was now gone and had been replaced with an arrogant, cheating piece of shit. One bitch, two bitch, three bitch, four bitch. I felt like the damn Cat in the

Hat. Every time I turned around, he was cheating with some funky, dusty, shit talking bitch. I wasn't catching him directly in the act. I'd go through his phone and there would be vague text messages or random phone calls. Every time I called or text a number back, it was a different chick. None of them would ever confirm anything. Nothing was ever concrete. I had no doubt that he was cheating; I just couldn't prove it. It was only when I had pure proof, that I gave his ass the boot. I would rather be alone than allow a nigga to treat me like shit. And I most definitely didn't want a nigga that had the gall to fuck another hoe in the bed we shared. There was no denying that I was bitter. Neal had shattered my heart and because of that I hated him and everything he stood for. I had given him two children and six years of my life when I could have been building with someone else. I was angry as fuck and I wasn't sure when that anger and pain was going to fade.

Despite all the hostility raging through me, I tapped Neal's number and called him back while I pumped my gas. Considering his girls and I were on the streets because of him, I was hoping that he set aside his petty ways and did right by us. I waited for the phone to ring, and once it did, Neal picked up on the second.

"Hello?" he asked, his deep voice filling my ears while he pretended not to know who it was calling. At one point that same voice would have sent my pussy in a fury, but now it was downright annoying. I honestly couldn't stand the sound of it.

"Your girls and I need a place to stay. I don't have enough money to pay up a hotel."

I didn't even bother blessing his raggedy ass with a hello. He knew it was me. He only had two children and I, of course, was the mother to both of them.

"Damn shawty. You can't answer the phone any other time, but you can hit a nigga when you need something. Being the fuck rude on top of it."

He let out a dry chuckle like I was unbelievable. I ain't gon' front, I had an attitude. I stayed with one because I usually had to interact with sorry ass people on the regular. Plus, I knew he was somewhere laid up in some bed-buggy bed, shaking his head, grinning because I'd finally called. I heard him shuffling around, then I heard a door close. He was probably hiding from whatever hoe he was laid up with. Although Neal had a few dollars and a car, he didn't have shit else. In the mere month that we'd been separated, I heard he'd been playing house with this bitch and that bitch while I ran around stressed the fuck out trying to keep a roof over his daughter's heads.

"Neal." I sighed.

I didn't have time for his silly ass games. I was about to hurry up and get his clown ass off my phone. Neal had a way about him. He was always smug and calm in the midst of chaos he caused, and it annoyed me.

"Are you going to bring me some money or not? You know I don't really have nobody else to stay with. The girls and I need somewhere to go. I'm about to take the last of our clothes to storage and then I want to check into a hotel or something until I figure out what's next."

He paused and then chuckled. "Figure out what's next, huh?"

"Yeah. I found a job at Walmart and I'm supposed to start next week. Once I get a few pay stubs along with the money I have saved, I'll be able to find a place."

"A job." Neal paused for a few seconds. "So, you really on some Ms. Independent shit. You really on some *fuck me* type shit," he grumbled, his mood noticeably souring.

"Neal, *you* said fuck us when you laid down with that dirty ass bitch in our bed. You and I are over. Now, are you gonna help me or fuckin not!" I snapped angrily. I glanced around the parking lot, hoping people hadn't heard my conversation.

"I ain't helping with shit! Since you don't fuck with a nigga and you got it all figured out, do that shit all by yo' mafuckin self," he countered. "And don't run around telling mafucka's that

7

I deny my girls. They got a place to stay. Take them to my mama house."

I went to speak but something told me to look down. The call had ended.

"This nigga hung up on me," I said quietly in disbelief.

His behavior was causing me to hate his ass even more. He knew I wasn't going to take them to his mother. I didn't have anything against her. She was a good grandmother; she just wasn't their mama. I was.

I finished pumping my gas and got back in the car. I threw the phone next to me on the passenger seat and shook my head. I didn't know why I was acting surprised. Neal had been feeling himself for a while. It was solely because of the money since he wasn't all that. Brown skinned with a slim physique; he wasn't nothing to write home about. The bitches he'd dated before me paled in comparison. Ironically, I only started dating Neal because he was regular. I always stayed away from dope boys because of my childhood. Most of them were arrogant and didn't give a fuck about nothing but money and treating others like they were beneath them.

I couldn't help but feel like I'd played myself. Him hanging up on me was the icing on the cake though. He was trying to teach me a lesson at the worst time. At my lowest point. The crazy part was I still loved Neal because of our history but I hated that motherfucker too because of the sorrow he put in my chest. *You got that nigga*, I thought to myself. He didn't have to worry about me asking him for a motherfuckin' thing else. If he thought I was going to cave in and go crawling back to him, he had me chopped. If he wanted to see me fold, then he could catch me at the laundromat.

"Mommy, where are we going?" my five-year-old and oldest daughter Sage asked me, yanking me away from my angry, negative thoughts. I looked back at my two girls, who were the spitting image of their father. Beautiful bronze skin, large eyes, and thick manes that resembled the Kanekalon hair you got from the corner store for a dollar, it was safe to say that they were traditional black beauties. Sage was the most inquisitive. Always observing and asking questions. My four-year-old, Violet, on the other hand, was laid back and didn't really care too much about nothing.

"Aunt Melva's," I said quickly before turning back around and doing my best to hide my disgruntled state. "I need you two to sit back and be quiet, okay? Mommy's trying to do something. I'm thinking right now."

"Okay," Sage and Violet replied in unison.

I took a deep breath. Aunt Melva's was the last place I wanted to be, but it didn't look like I had much choice.

## ✻ 2 ✻

## ALIZE

After losing my apartment, the girls and I moved in with Aunt Melva. We'd only been there a few days, but it felt like a century. It was a warm, Thursday night in June and since Aunt Melva stayed on a quiet block, I let the girls run themselves ragged outside in the yard. It was a small luxury to them, since other than the occasional visits to the park downtown, they didn't go outside.

After ripping and running for the latter part of the day, I finally had them settled down, bathed and was tucking them into the full-size bed we shared, when I heard my phone chirp on the nearby nightstand. I reached over and grabbed it to see I had a text message from my cousin Melvina, my aunt Melva's daughter.

**Hey my favorite cousin**!

A smirk crept up on my face. I knew her ass wanted something when she hit me with that favorite cousin line.

**Hey girl. Wassup?**

I waited for her to respond, but after thirty seconds, my phone began to vibrate in my hand, informing me that I had an incoming call. I silenced it completely but saw that it was Melvina calling me. I figured whatever she had to tell me was too much to put in a text. I glanced at my girls who were snuggled against one another, looking peaceful. I couldn't help but smile as I stood to my feet. They were my world.

"Goodnight girls. I'm going downstairs to sit with Aunt Melva. I'm not leaving," I assured them before hitting the light switch, walking out the room, and closing the door behind me.

Sage nor Violet could stand being at Aunt Melva's. Children could often peep character and vibes before most adults could. In Aunt Melva's case, they were spot on. At only four and five, they'd already revealed that they flat out didn't like her and that she was mean. They'd be ready to cause a fuss if they even thought for a second that I was about to leave them there with her. They could care less that it was their bedtime, and they were going to be sleeping. They were used to being by my side unless I was out looking for a job. Any other time, I kept them with me.

Since the girls and I shared a room on the second floor, I made my way gently down the steps and began heading through the living room to get to the front door. I was going to stand on the porch and call Melvina back. It was just my luck that my Aunt Melva was sprawled out on the sofa watching television as I walked through.

"And where is you about to go?" her nosy ass asked with a slight attitude.

I stopped at the end of the steps and responded. "I'm just taking a call on the porch really quick. I didn't want to disturb the girls."

"Well, I don't want you disturbing me either, opening and closing my door. Ain't nothing changed. My door still locks at the same time," she reminded me with her lips pursed together.

Aunt Melva was a fair-skinned woman who was petite in stature and wore a short, dry, nappy ass afro on top of her head. To the untrained eye, she looked sweet as pumpkin pie; however, to those that knew her, she was mean as a junkyard dog.

"And what time is that Aunt Melva? It's been a while," I told her, drawing in a deep, silent breath to keep from inadvertently matching her negative ass energy.

"Eight o'clock, unless you're going to or from work."

She knew damn well that I didn't have a job and wasn't scheduled to start working until the following week.

"You got a few minutes," she said after glancing down at her watch. The whole time she spoke, she never took her eyes off the TV.

"Okay," I said flatly, before heading out the door.

I loved my aunt but a large part of me couldn't stand her. In my opinion, she was mean, miserable, and just plain ol' money-hungry. I remembered my mom saying similar shit back in the day, but at the time I was too young to comprehend. I moved in with Aunt Melva right after my hospital visit because of the Rat Bite Fever I'd caught. When the worker assigned to my case called her, she didn't hesitate to swoop in and save the day. She'd take me in, knowing full-well that my mother would never get the treatment she needed to get better and provide me a safe and stable living environment.

I ended up staying with Aunt Melva until I turned eighteen and moved out. And trust me when I say, I had wanted to leave long before that. I couldn't lie, when I first moved in with my aunt, I was in heaven. Hot meals, hot baths and a warm bed were all foreign to me. She was stern but in a loving way. Melvina and I were around the same age, so I had someone to play with, and although I missed my mom, I was happy. In the beginning, my caseworker was in and out doing home visits, making sure I was well cared for. Of course, Aunt Melva was always on her best behavior, had a fridge full of food, and kept the house immaculate even though we were in the hood. Eventually, those home visits from my caseworker slowed until finally they became non-existent. That's when Aunt Melva seemed to do a three-sixty.

Aunt Melva would go from being stern and loving to down-right mean. It was never physical abuse, usually just verbal. It was like she really looked down on me because I had come from the womb of a crackhead. Any reason she had to make fun of me, she would. If I left a plate in the sink, I was a Viking or

Barbarian. If I didn't clean up good enough, I was a dirty ass who was used to living in filth. Anytime I fucked up, it was always, "like mother, like child." From the moment those monitored visits stopped, I wasn't good enough. The bitch would even make fun of the scars left from the bite marks I'd gotten.

I eventually realized Aunt Melva never helped me out of love. She just had me for the check. I would get basics while she essentially lived off the bulk of the money that she received for me. I wore hair store flats and sandals while Melvina wore Jordan's and Nikes. I dressed in Goodwill shit while Melvina shopped in the malls. The crazy part was, I was so used to nothing that I didn't even complain. Aunt Melva had my mind warped where I was thankful for the smallest of things. People in the neighborhood used to whisper about how she treated me differently, but I never told anyone at school or informed my constantly changing caseworkers. I was just thankful to have a roof over my head and a bed of my own. When I met Neal and he showed me what I thought was "real" love, I rolled the fuck out the day after I turned eighteen. I visited out of respect, but I hadn't been back to live since.

Shaking off Aunt Melva's negativity when I got on the porch, I dug my phone out my pocket and called Melvina back.

"Hey girl," I greeted her, when she picked up.

"Damn bitch. I thought you had fell asleep. As long as it took you to call me back."

"Naw girl. I had just put the girls to bed and then I was talking to yo' mama."

I left out the part about her getting the fuck on my nerves. Even though Aunt Melva treated me the way she did, she was actually a decent mother to Melvina. Sadly, she was blind to her mother's ways at times.

"Oh, okay. So, look, I need a huge favor," Melvina said, jumping right into the reason she had called.

"And what favor is that?" I asked curiously as I leaned against the side of the house.

"I need you to ride out with me. "

"Ride out where?"

She paused for a moment and it was then that I knew she was about to say some crazy shit. "Vegas."

"Vegas!" I repeated to make sure I'd heard what I heard. "Bitch, you know I can't take off and go all the way to no damn Vegas at the last minute. I don't even have a crib right now. I'm supposed to start working in a few days. I can't do that," I told her with finality.

My poor choices and actions had already landed my girls without a place to stay; I had to be responsible.

"Well hear me out before you say no," she pleaded. "You know I wouldn't call you with no bullshit unless it benefited you in some kind of way."

"Talk."

"So, you know niggas stay all up in my inbox. Most of the time, you know I don't even be reading them messages. But the other day I got one from a nigga named Murder Maine. This motherfucker got a couple dollars, so I figured I'd entertain the nigga for a brief second to see what type of time he on."

"You talking 'bout the rapper nigga from Cali?"

I'd heard of him. He was a butt-ugly, up-and-coming light-skinned rapper with a mouth full of stinky ass golds and a social media account full of dope music. Murder Maine wasn't attractive in any way, shape, or form, but he was talented and flashy, and that was enough for chicks like my cousin who lacked substance. Don't get it twisted, I loved Melvina. She was a ton of fun and had a crazy sense of humor. However, she was conceited, vain, had no morals, and she would do just about anything for a dollar. Her strength was the average person couldn't tell all that from a couple encounters. She let niggas know they couldn't step to her unless they had funds, but she still came across as sweet, warm and caring. In reality, she couldn't give two fucks about anyone or anything. Despite her slithery, snaky ways, it seemed to be working for her. Melvina had a small but luxurious condo in downtown Atlanta and drove a new model Audi. She bought all the latest designers like Balenciaga, Gucci, and Chanel.

"You listening?" she asked, snatching me out of my thoughts.

"I didn't hear you. Repeat it please."

Melvina let out a huff then proceeded to repeat what I had missed. "The nigga hit me up and wants to fly me out to Vegas. Him and a few of his homies went out there to gamble and shit for the weekend."

"So, what does that have to do with me, Vina?"

"He wants me to bring a friend."

"Well find one to take. I ain't yo' friend no way bitch. I'm your cousin."

It was the truth. Melvina and I hardly ever hung out. We hadn't hung out since teenagers except here and there at a family function. Melvina was a few years older than me. She moved out as soon as she graduated high school and immediately began running the streets, mingling amongst entertainers and models. Two Brazilian Butt Lift's later and a couple rich dick's up in her and she hardly fucked with me. I was boring and basic to her. She'd never actually said that, but I knew that's what it was. I found me a little nigga, settled down and had a couple kids. The bitches she fucked with were bougie and I didn't like hoes around me that I had to watch.

"What happened to that bitch you used to hang with? Alexis?"

Alexis was another big-booty, "so-called" Instagram model that dated ballers all the while whispering sweet-nothings and spewing lies into their ears. I couldn't lie, she definitely was a baddie though.

"Girl fuck her. That hoe done found her a rich nigga and done got knocked the fuck up so she's out of commission. I can't hate on her though. She definitely came up," she said before growing quiet and giving me the opportunity to reply.

"So, hypothetically speaking, if I did go with you, what's in it for me?" I asked. Melvina was about her money so I knew somewhere up in the conversation, it was going to come up, but I wanted her to hurry up and get the fuck to it.

"Airfare paid. Hotel room paid. And as soon as we land, he gon' wire me five racks."

"Sounds like somebody fuckin' and it ain't gon' be me," I unintentionally spat out.

I mean, I could have been wrong, but most niggas weren't coming off racks unless a chick was giving up something.

"Girl, whatever. I'll give you two of that five if you come with me. That's a quick and easy two grand. You don't gotta do shit but show up, look cute and laugh and grin in a few niggas face. I know you need it," she eased in.

As much as I wanted to tell her 'hell naw', she was right. I did need it. I was poor for real. I had four-hundred dollars in my bank account and a quarter tank of gas in my used Hyundai. A few racks would help put me in a new apartment.

"Make it half and you gotta deal." I knew that if Melvina was flying to Vegas for five thousand dollars upfront, then she was going to finesse the nigga out some more bread. I also knew that the bulk of the cash she gave me was going to have to go right to a babysitter.

"Half?" she scoffed.

"Yeah, half hoe. I'm gonna have to pay Aunt Melva to watch the girls ... *and* you're gonna be the one to ask her. When does the flight leave?" I asked.

"Soon. It's a red eye. It leaves at three." I shook my head. I had no doubt I was her last resort. She was literally giving me a few hours' notice. Lucky for her, I so desperately needed the money.

"Call Aunt Melva and I'll start packing."

⚜

"I love you, Sage. I love you, Violet," I cooed into the phone to each one of my girls individually. I missed my babies already.

Since I'd had them, I'd never gone more than a few hours away from them. I didn't have any friends, my mother was dead, and Aunt Melva babysitting for me was usually out of the question.

The flight from Atlanta to Las Vegas lasted around four hours. I usually loved traveling but since I was leaving my girls, I wasn't as chipper as I should have been. As soon as we touched down, I was calling Aunt Melva so I could speak with them. I told them that I was away for a day for work and asked them to behave. I'd let my aunt slide with how she treated me, but I wasn't letting shit slide about my children. That was the main reason that she was watching them for the very first time. Since I pushed them out, I vowed to protect them and trust me when I say, I would step about my babies. I had gone through Hell as a child, and I refused to let that happen with mine.

After saying bye to my kids, Melvina and I caught an Uber to Caesar's Palace, where we were staying for the one night we were there. Although I expected to stay in a nice hotel, I wasn't expecting one like that. Neal had never really taken me anywhere nice so I couldn't lie, I was impressed with a lot shit that was outside of the projects. There were several restaurants on site, a casino, several pools, all of them surrounded by Spanish-looking architecture. A spa. Shit, there was even a colosseum. Atlanta had some bomb ass hotels, but I'd never seen anything like the one we were staying in. When we got to our room, it was spacious with an exotic looking jacuzzi and a king-size bed that I assumed Melvina and I would be sharing. Everything was great, but I had a burning question that I couldn't hold in. I just had to get it out since noticing some shit at the front desk.

"Vina, why that nigga got the room in his name?" I finally asked.

When we arrived at the front desk to check in, I was surprised to see that the room had already been checked in under a Jermaine Bivens. I quickly concluded that the name belonged to none other than Murder Maine.

Melvina shrugged. "Girl, to be honest, I don't even ask a lot of questions. I just show up. It's only for one night though so I ain't trippin' 'bout it."

I shot her a quick glance and felt my face inadvertently frown up. Because of her lack of questioning, we weren't listed on the room as registered guests, which could go terribly wrong if Vina and the nigga Murda Maine got into it for any reason. He could literally put us out or take us off his registration card. I wasn't even about to make a big stink about it though. Melvina got flown out all the time so I had faith in the fact that she knew what she was doing. Besides, she had already given me half of the twenty-five-hundred-dollars that she'd promised. I was going to get the rest in a few hours. Vina was definitely about her coins and proved to be a woman of her word. Almost, anyway. Initially, she had told me that I would get the full amount as soon as we landed, but according to her, Murda Maine switched things up.

Settling in our room, we got comfortable and made plans for the day. Since it was still early when we checked in, we both went to sleep for roughly six-hours. After showering and eating a late lunch at one of the restaurants on site, we walked around for about an hour and did a little sightseeing. The entire time, Murda Maine was blowing Melvina's phone up.

"Girl, this nigga is so thirsty," she groaned as we walked the lively Vegas strip. I was enjoying myself, but my face was still balled up into a frown because the brutal Nevada sun was cutting into my skin like razor blades.

"He ready to hang out?" I asked, adjusting the wide brim straw hat I'd purchased last-minute in a desperate attempt to defend myself against the sun.

"Yeah. They already down at the casino spending money. They're going to grab a table for dinner before we come down. We'll meet them in the restaurant."

"Good, because it's hot as fuck out here," I complained.

People always bragged about how Vegas was lit but they never mentioned the dry ass heat.

"Bitch, what you expect? It's the fuckin' desert. Use your

brain." Melvina rolled her eyes and then followed it up with a friendly laugh.

I saw the smile, but I didn't find shit funny. I hated insults disguised as jokes. She was good for that and so was her mother.

"True, but I didn't fuckin' know," I countered.

"Girl, don't get all defensive. Let's grab some ice cream and head back to this hotel because you're right; it is hot out as Satan's lair out this bitch."

After grabbing our ice cream, Melvina and I got back to the hotel about twenty-minutes later and began getting dressed. She went into the bathroom first, while I laid back on the bed, checked in on my kids and skimmed through the texts and missed calls that Neal had sent me. I didn't respond to any of the shit he'd sent since there wasn't much to say. He talked stupid most of the time anyway.

According to him, I was making it worse on me and the kids by being stubborn and prideful. A lot of dizzy bitches would have agreed. Yeah, it would have been easier to just take Neal back so I could be in a new place with my girls, but I wasn't even about to pretend that I wanted his ass any longer. I deserved better. I had been getting treated like shit all my life. Since I was a kid. I was finally an adult and that shit was over.

Despite feeling like I was doing the right thing, a large part of me did feel like I was being selfish. My children didn't deserve to be without a place, and I had the opportunity to get them in one quickly. But then I told myself that they also deserved to be in a healthy, loving home. A home that would allow them to set high standards for themselves later in life. Yeah, I was struggling, but my girls and I had a warm bed and a roof over our head for the moment. I was done letting Neal manipulate and control me by dangling basic necessities in my face. Sage, Violet, and I were going to be just fine without Neal's ass. Period. I would never deny him the ability to see his children, but he was going to have to grow the fuck up if he wanted to be in their lives.

After taking forever, Melvina finally emerged from the bathroom with a thick towel wrapped around her torso. That was my cue. Grabbing my things, I went in directly behind her and began working on my own hygiene.

About an hour later, I was done getting dressed and made up. Tossing back a silky strand of hair out the front of my face, I admired myself in the bathroom mirror. The racy white, one-shoulder bodycon dress squeezed my frame closely and tastefully. I looked sexy but I didn't look like I was trying too hard. I had even washed and dried my hair before flat ironing it, giving it a slick look. A little concealer, mascara, and a heavy hand of lip gloss and I was ready to step out. Couldn't nobody tell me I didn't look like a snack.

"Alize you ready!" I heard my cousin impatiently yell out from the bedroom. Still standing in front of the mirror, I watched my reflection immediately transform. My lip curled upwards, and my eyes slid around in a circle. She had asked me was I ready twice already.

"Yeah! Here I come," I called out. She had the nerve to be trying to rush me when she was the one who had tied the bathroom up for the longest. She was supposed to take her time doing whatever the fuck she was doing, and I was supposed to rush? I didn't think so. She had me confused with her flunky Alexis. I let go of my annoyed state, pushed open the door and emerged from the bathroom all smiles.

"How do I look?" I asked, my smile dissolving from my face as soon as my gaze landed on her.

She was standing by the bed and had turned around to face me when I walked out. I couldn't lie, she instantly had me feeling super basic. My eyes wandered her voluptuous body from head to toe. She had on a neon green bandage dress that exposed her non-existent waist, washboard stomach and melon-like implants. Her face had been flawlessly made up and her bonnet had been removed to reveal a thirty-inch weave that had been perfectly pressed so that it now clung to her backside. She was drop-dead gorgeous. An undeniable ten.

"You look cute," Melvina said, sounding genuine, although a part of me couldn't help but feel that she was just being nice.

"Come on. We gotta roll though. We already had these niggas waiting long enough, and he done texted and called me over a dozen times."

"Vina, why you ain't tell me you were getting this dolled up? I feel underdressed," I whined, my confident attitude dwindling by the second.

"Girl, you're fine. You know I always be doing the most," she said before waving me to follow behind her.

I grabbed my purse off my self-designated side of the bed and reluctantly followed behind her. I was low-key pissed that she didn't tell me that she was going all out on her attire and makeup. There I was looking "around the way girl fly," and she was looking like a fuckin' Instagram model. When I asked her if my outfit was okay earlier that day, she downplayed it like we were going to be on some lounging in the casino type shit. However, she was dressed like she was about to go on an expensive night out on the town. Had I known that, I would have ran into a boutique or something and grabbed a fit more appropriate. Exhaling a deep breath, I followed her out the door. Hearing my not-so-subtle sigh, she turned around and asked me, "You okay?"

"Yeah, I'm fine."

"Good. Now, let's go get this money."

🕉

"It's about damn time!" Murda Maine said drunkenly and obnoxiously as we approached their round table booth in the restaurant, Amalfi by Bobby Flay.

He was right; we'd definitely taken a long time. The upscale restaurant was right inside of Caesar's Palace and even though Murda Maine was tired of waiting, it was an inappropriate place for him to be acting all loud and ghetto in. I, of course, recognized him right away to be the rapper since I knew his face from Instagram, and he was also the one wearing the biggest, shiniest jewelry indicating that he was the one with the money out the bunch. Every time he moved, his large, chunky chain swung with him. It was definitely glistening and gleaming no matter which way it curved.

"We didn't mean to keep y'all waiting but we had to get cute," Melvina said nonchalantly.

She stood at the edge of the table and flashed everyone seated a smile. I expected a small entourage, but Murda Maine only had two others with them. They were also light-bright and looked like they were likely related to him. They were both well-dressed and didn't appear as intoxicated as the rapper.

"Y'all gonna make some room or have us standing here?" Melvina asked.

"Oh, shit. My bad. Y'all niggas move over. Make room for the ladies," Murda Maine said, flashing a gold smile.

Even though the golds in his mouth were supposed to indicate his wealth, it wasn't a good look for him. As light as he was, the golds made him look like he simply had a mouth full of big, yellow-ass teeth. I told myself that I was going to be on my best behavior though. Lately, my temper hadn't been the best. I'd been really sensitive and short, and I didn't want it to affect the night. After the men slid over, Melvina and I sat down and scooted in.

"This is my cousin Alize," she said, introducing me to the three fuckin' stooges. That was my nickname for them since I had a feeling the night was going to be a laughable one. The table was piled up with a bunch of empty shot glasses and a few bottles. I had to wonder why the waitress or waiter hadn't come and taken any of them off. Then I realized that they were probably being rude and annoying, so no one wanted to deal with them.

"Yo' name Alize like the drink?" Murda Maine asked.

"Yeah. Like the drink." I nodded and smiled, doing my best to appear flirty and sociable.

"Oh okay. Yo' mama probably used to be lit back in the day. She named her daughter after a fuckin' cheap ass bottle of liquor," he said before cackling.

My eyes narrowed, and Melvina nudged me.

"Yeah, something like that. Are there any extra menus?" I asked. I was hungry and I really wanted him to shut the fuck up.

"Nah. These motherfuckers ain't bring us none. Just the drink menu. You want that?" he asked before tossing it in front of us, damn near striking Melvina in the face with it. I sighed inwardly. It was going to be a long night.

"Oh, I'm Maine."

He smiled proudly after finally introducing himself.

"These two niggas is my left hand and my right hand." He pointed to his left. "This my cousin Billy." He pointed to his right. "This my brother Ruger."

"How y'all doing?" I flashed the both of them a soft smile before looking over at the drink menu that Melvina was holding.

"We need a real menu with some food on it. We hungry." Melvina tossed the menu to the side and began looking around for a server. I could tell that she was doing her best to get the night going on a good start.

"Waiter!!!!!" Maine shrieked at the top of his lungs, surprising everyone at our tables and others around.

"Yo, chill the fuck out." His brother Ruger laughed and nudged him with his elbow. He then directed his attention back on us. "This nigga trippin'."

Before I could respond, our waitress appeared, looking all anxious like she was ready to leave just as she got there.

"What can I get for you ladies?" she asked with a friendly smile, although I could tell that she wanted nothing to do with the men at the table.

"I'll take a Sangria," I told her. I didn't drink heavy, but I knew I was going to need something – anything, to make it through the night with Maine's foolishness.

"Alright." The waitress nodded and then turned to Melvina.

"Double shot of Hennessy for me."

"Alright. I'll be right back with those drinks for you ladies."

"Bring me another bottle of D'Ussé," Maine demanded before she could fully walk off.

"I'm sorry. But I was told that I wasn't able to serve you guys any more alcohol. I don't make the rules, I just follow them," she said politely before scurrying off.

"She told you that already nigga," Billy said with a frown while shaking his head at Maine. I could tell that they were just as fed up with his ass as everyone else. "When you visibly fucked up, they can't keep serving you alcohol, making you worse."

"This nigga been drinking all fucking day," Ruger tried to explain. "He gets like this when we take trips. Just enjoying life. So, don't pay this nigga no mind," he said.

I could tell that Billy and Ruger stayed by Maine's side to keep him from crashing like the dummy he was. And although I heard Ruger tell me not to pay him no mind, I didn't respond. My expression had soured because of the way Maine was just yelling, spitting and carrying on. He was fucking embarrassing.

"He good," Melvina said, flashing Maine a seductive smile. "I'll calm his ass down by the end of the night."

"I bet you will," he grinned back, sticking his tongue out his mouth seductively.

"Ugh," I accidentally said aloud. I didn't know why I always did that shit. My brain just did its own thing. I could be thinking something and somehow it would find its way right out my mouth.

"What the fuck you mean *ugh*, bitch?" Maine spat defensively.

My eyes narrowed again. This time to slits.

"Excuse me?"

"Yo chill, Maine. Please don't pay him no mind," Ruger tried to reason again.

That time however, I didn't want to hear that shit. The nigga had already come out his mouth disrespectful once. There weren't any more passes being given.

"I'm trying to figure out who the fuck you talkin' too?" I asked him just as the waiter had returned with our drinks. She noticed the hostility, so she quickly sat our drinks down in front of us and took off.

Maine stopped and stared at me through his glossy eyes, his mouth agape. I guess he wasn't used to no female checking him or talking to him that way. He turned to Melvina and drunkenly said, "Why did you even bring this hoe? Where did you find her? I damn sure ain't kick out five racks for no little, broke block bitch."

"Maine, chill. That's my cousin," Melvina pleaded with him.

I turned and glanced at her. I was ready to go.

"Fuck that nigga. I'm out, Vina. You can sit down here with this drunk disrespectful shit all night but I'm not."

I took a sip of my drink for the road but began getting up so I could roll. Melvina tugged on my arm, pulling me back down so she could say something. She leaned into my ear and whispered.

"Bitch I'm giving you twenty-five hundred to deal with it."

I couldn't help but laugh out loud and shake my head at what she just said.

"You can keep that. I showed up. I got half and I'm going back to the room."

Maine smacked his teeth and threw his hand up, waving me off as if I were some peasant, while other patrons of the restaurant looked at us.

"Fuck her. Let her go," he said to Melvina.

"And bitch, you cute but you ain't all that no mafucking way."

"What nigga?" I snapped, my neck rolling to meet Maine's ugly ass gaze.

"You heard me. You sitting here acting all funky and stuck up like you better than niggas. You average at best lil' baby," he called himself informing me. "What's that dress? Fashion Nova?" He laughed.

Maine then turned his attention to Melvina and continued to talk his shit.

"I told you to bring a bad bitch. Like the broad you usually be with on Instagram. Not some stuck-up, dry acting, basic bitch that can't take a fucking joke."

The saying was, 'the truth hurts'. Whoever came up with it was right because the words that rolled off Murda Maine's lips had sliced through me. Maybe I was basic sitting next to Melvina with her caked-on makeup, and big, hard ass, no shade to my cousin. But he didn't have to put that shit so brutally. In his eyes and from his own mouth, I was a basic, broke, block bitch with a ghetto ass name. I was pissed, and even though the sweet-tasting glass of Sangria I was drinking was too good to spit out, I couldn't control the urge I had to waste the rest.

Before Maine could utter another insult, I threw the full glass right into his face. That night wasn't like the night I shot at Neal and Melissa. Nah. That night, my aim was perfect. When I snatched the glass off the table and chucked it into Maine's grinning face, it landed perfectly. Of course, he didn't waste any time hopping up and lunging at me while his folks rolled around laughing at his ass. It wasn't me throwing the drink in his face that was the most comical part. It was how furious, discombobulated, and foolish his ass was after the fact.

"Bitch, I'm gon' break yo' fuckin' neck!" he shrieked. His face was dripping wet with Sangria, and he was flailing around, damn near knocking everything off the table onto the ground to get to where I was now standing. His white Gucci shirt was stained red and was clinging to his frail chest.

"You not gon' do shit!" I yelled, purposely drawing more attention to the table.

I knew security would be rolling up in a few more seconds. In the meantime, Ruger and Billy had hopped up and were pulling him back so he couldn't get to me. Maine was so mad, his face was flushed, veins were creeping up the sides of his neck, and he was damn near foaming at the mouth. He was definitely a little intimidating but if he got too close to me, I was going to bash him across his fucking head with the liquor bottle I had grabbed off the table after throwing my drink into his face.

"I told you I wanted to fucking leave!" I turned and yelled at Melvina.

I didn't wait for her to reply. I stormed away from the table and headed out of the restaurant. I spun around when I felt someone snatch my arm back.

"Get the fuck off me!" I yelled out before realizing it was Melvina and turning it down a notch.

"Yo what the fuck is up with you!" she argued as she stood in front of me with a scowl and hands on her big, thick hips.

My attitude hadn't been initially directed at her, but since she wanted to run up on me with a little too much bass in her voice, I immediately got defensive. We were both now standing at the entrance of the restaurant looking like we were about to go head up.

"Girl fuck that nigga! You asked me to come with you, laugh, joke and flirt. Not get disrespected and fucking insulted! I left my own nigga because of that! What makes you think I'm gon' put up with that shit from another nigga I don't even know?"

"You gon' fuck up your money for some harmless jokes from a nigga that isn't important?" she asked.

I was about ready to smack the shit out of Melvina. She was lucky she was my cousin, plus I knew that she could fight a little bit.

"Wasn't nothing about them jokes harmless, Vina. None of the jokes were on you. I hope you got the rest of yo' money. I ain't putting up with that shit for a couple dollars."

"And that's exactly why you don't got shit and you fuckin' broke!" she spat cruelly, catching me off guard.

"What?" My hands tightened into fists at my side. I didn't

have a drink to throw but I was getting ready to throw hands if she said some more fly shit.

"You broke because you too fucking sensitive. Shouldn't be no pride when you fucked up and a nigga sitting in front of you ready and willing to bless you," she pointed in my face angrily.

"Vina, get yo' hand out my motherfuckin' face or we gon' fight. And that's on my dead mama," I threatened.

She rolled her eyes but brought her hand down before she addressed me. She knew I didn't put shit on my mama unless I meant it.

"Shake that pride shit cuz, or you never gon' have shit. I'm 'bout to go back and get this money. That nigga drunk ... and trust and believe, I'll have an extra couple racks in my pocket for that disrespect. You see, I don't get all mad and hype about shit that's out of my control. I don't get out of character, shooting at motherfuckers and risking what I have. You need to learn that you can't always get even ... but you can always get paid. And believe me, I can show you better than I can tell you. I'll see you later," she told me before turning back around and sashaying her big, fake ass back into the restaurant.

I didn't bother responding. I turned back around and headed in the opposite direction so I could get back to the room. Since I already had half of my money, I figured I would grab my things and roll. Fuck Melvina. I was going to go get me a cheap little room somewhere close by and then catch an Uber to the airport in the morning. As long as I had my belongings and my plane ticket, I was good.

As usual though, I had the worst luck. When I got back upstairs to the room, the pussy nigga, Maine must have already called to the front desk and had them deactivate the keys. After inserting mine into the room's key slot several times and having it rejected, I realized I wasn't getting into the room.

"Fuck!" I shouted.

Out of frustration, I screamed again at the top of my lungs in the fancy ass hotel and then kicked the door. My duffel bag with my clothes were still in the room. All I had was my purse. Luckily, that contained my wallet, driver's license and plane ticket. Feeling helpless, I got back on the elevator and went down to speak with someone at the front desk.

"What can I do for you?" the chipper, front-desk clerk asked. She was an attractive, middle-age white-woman. Since she was in a good mood, I figured she just might be the one to help me get my things so I could be on my way. It was worth a shot anyway.

"Umm, hi." I forced a tight smile. I figured I might as well be honest. "I'm in room 406. My key isn't working. I'm not asking to be let back in the room because I know that the registered guest of the room probably called and had the keys deactivated. We had a little disagreement and I'm trying to leave, but I need my things out of the room. Is there any way that someone can go in the room and just grab my duffel bag and give it to me so I can be on my way?" I asked sweetly,

"I'll see what I can do," she said, her expression changing from chipper to a little more serious. "Give me one-minute, ma'am."

She focused on her computer screen, navigating her mouse around and occasionally giving it a click. After about thirty-seconds, she paused for a minute and began reading what were probably notes. She rose up from her seat and told me that she would be right back. Turning her back to me, she walked through a door that separated the large front desk area from what was probably a back office. While I waited patiently for her to return, I stood there nervously and tried to call Melvina. All I wanted were my things. If I couldn't get them, then I was just going to ask her to grab them for me.

The first time I called, the phone rang once and then went directly to voicemail. The second time it didn't ring at all; it just went directly to voicemail again. I let out a grunt and put my phone back in my purse. *This fuck ass bitch*, I thought to myself. After that second call, I quickly realized that she wasn't going to answer. Melvina would often get in her ways and would ignore someone quick. I wasn't about to keep calling her though. Even if I couldn't get my things, I was going to chalk it up as a loss and head out. After waiting about a minute, the front-desk clerk returned. From her expression, I knew that she wasn't going to be able to help me.

"Thank you so much for waiting." She then shot me a sympathetic look. "I spoke to my manager and you are right. The registered owner of the room doesn't want anyone going in or out. The keys have been deactivated, and he's going to come up and get new ones. I, nor anyone else, is able to go into the room and bother any of the belongings. I'm so sorry."

I shook my head and blew out a frustrated breath. I wasn't even going to take my irritation out on her. She had been very nice to me and was simply doing her job. I decided to say fuck the duffel bag and leave it.

"It's okay. Thanks for trying," I said to her before walking away from the front desk and out of the hotel. I dug my phone out my purse, scheduled an Uber and then texted Melvina.

**You a sorry bitch. How you gonna choose that fuck nigga over your own family. You could have easily found some more dick to suck. You don't gotta ever worry about me again.**

I hit send and then went to her contact information and blocked her. I also went to all my social media pages and blocked her there. I didn't want to hear shit that bitch had to say ever again.

After getting dropped off at the cheap room I'd booked last-minute online, I settled in, checked on my kids one last time, and went to sleep. Our returning flight was scheduled for six in the morning, so I figured I'd catch a little snooze beforehand. Unfortunately, when the time came for me to leave, my trip to Vegas went from bad to worse.

"What do you mean my flight's been canceled?" I asked the lady at the Delta desk the next day, after she slid my crumpled-up confirmation letter that Vina had printed out and given me.

"Your flight's been canceled. Whoever booked the flight called and canceled it."

"How can she cancel *my* flight?" I felt like I was losing air to my lungs and my chest began to get tight. Just when I thought things couldn't get any worse for me, I had been proved wrong.

"Ma'am ... the flight was under my name," I told her for clarity.

"I know that sweetheart, but this is something that I see a lot. Someone else made the reservation and because someone else made the reservation, they have the ability to modify it. Whoever made this reservation, *canceled* it," she said with emphasis.

"Well can you tell me if there is still a flight on the reservation at all?"

"I checked that already as well, and yes, it is. There were two flights on the reservation. One was canceled and the other one remains. The date was changed on the second one but it's still there."

I couldn't believe what was happening to me. I had one last question for her though.

"Are you able to tell me who made the reservation? Was it Melvina McKoy?"

I honestly felt stupid that I had never asked those questions to begin with. I trusted Melvina so I didn't question her.

"Yes, it was," she stated without even going back to the computer to check. I knew she was telling the truth. When I had gotten to the airport earlier and tried to print my boarding pass, I ran into issues. Because of those issues, I went to the desk and had them pull up my name to find my flight and reservation information. She searched the computer system high and low until she found out was going on.

Hearing her confirm that Melvina had canceled my reservation was all that I needed to know.

"Okay. Well can I purchase a new ticket here through you?" I asked her, moving forward in defeat. I would deal with Melvina's ass later when I ran into her. And I was going to make it my business to run into her.

"Yes, you can. You want the same flight?" she asked.

"Yes, please." I waited while she shuffled around her computer and attempted to honor my request. After watching her facial expression change a few times, I prepared myself to hear some more bullshit.

"That flight unfortunately, can't take any more passengers. It's sold out. The next flight leaves later today but it's four-hundred-eighty-six dollars."

"What!" I said a little too loudly, drawing attention from others in the line, waiting for me to get the hell out the way.

"I'm so sorry. It's a little expensive because it's last minute. Most of the flights are sold out."

I sighed. I didn't have a choice. I paid for the ticket and then took it when she printed it out and handed it to me. As I was walking off, I glanced down at my ticket and stopped. The times didn't make sense to me. There must had been some type of mistake. The ticket I was holding said my flight was eight fucking hours. With a departure time of four in the afternoon, I wasn't scheduled to arrive until after midnight.

"Umm, Miss. There must be a mistake," I said, quickly walking back and cutting off the next customer heading to the counter. "This says the flight is going to take over eight hours. "It's only a four-hour flight from here to Atlanta."

"That's no mistake. That flight has two stops."

"So, you mean to tell me there's a layover?"

She nodded. "Yes. That's the only flight available left for today, ma'am."

I shook my head and walked off in disgust. I didn't bother saying anything else since there wasn't anything that she nor I could do. I was already leaving way past schedule, meaning Aunt Melva had to keep the girls longer than originally agreed upon. An eight-hour flight was basically adding on another entire day. Aunt Melva's greedy ass was already making me give her five-hundred-dollars to watch the girls for one day. I didn't want to agree to it but Melvina had to tell her what I was up to and what I was getting in order to get her to agree to keep them. Realizing it was a quick come-up for everyone involved, she agreed while setting that hefty price tag.

As I settled in a chair in the waiting area, I called Aunt Melva and told her what happened and that I was coming back late. I also told her how her sorry-ass daughter had done me, hoping that she would cut me some slack on the babysitting fee. I didn't know why I thought that. Aunt Melva didn't give a single fuck about any of what I told her. Since I was going to be gone an extra day, the fee had doubled. According to her, I now owed her a thousand dollars.

"Aunt Melva I can't pay you that," I argued. "Melvina only gave me twelve-hundred-fifty-dollars. She canceled my flight which forced me to get a last-minute flight that cost nearly five-hundred."

"I watched your kids and that's what we agreed upon per day. Y'all disagreement don't have anything to do with me. If you can't give me a thousand dollars, y'all gon' have to leave my house when you get back," she said with no remorse.

"I'll make sure you get your money," I lied, before hanging up.

I was so angry I was shaking in my seat. I felt like she was trying to take advantage of me. My girls weren't even bad. They had probably been sitting in the room all day not bothering her at all. She was just fucking greedy. Always had been and always would be.

Aunt Melva wasn't getting a grand from me. If I paid her that, I would be dipping into the little four hundred dollars that I had in my savings account before I flew out to Vegas. I was tired of motherfuckers treating me like I was weak as fuck. I'd been shown by too many people, countless times, that they didn't give a fuck about me. It was time to show everyone else that I didn't need them and that if they wanted to be dirty, then I could be the same way.

## 3

# LANCE

"I don't care how you put it, you can't be warring with no average, square ass nigga," I argued with my younger brother Lawrence.

In my opinion, he was twenty-five going on four. He was a hot head that never thought things through, usually always acting purely off emotions. I understood it because it was a flaw that I too had struggled with in the past; however, I had learned long ago that if one couldn't control their emotions then their emotions would certainly control them.

"Man fuck that nigga!" he snapped, apparently losing the little patience he did have. "He wanna talk shit like a mafuckin gangsta, so I'm gonna treat him like he one. We match energy 'round here," Lawrence continued to argue back.

If I were a bitch, I probably would've rolled my eyes, but since I wasn't, I just paused and drew in a deep breath. Back in the day, I would have agreed with my brother; however, after catching my first body at sixteen and then going to war behind it, resulting in catching nearly a dozen more, I learned to think. I would kill if I had to, but I hated beefing about senseless shit. As a grown man, I would sit down and talk that shit out. I wasn't above communicating. Taking a life changed people. It had certainly changed me.

"We can't keep letting niggas get away with talking crazy and doing fuck shit," he stressed.

He sounded stupid. He was talking about a popular NBA star named Blaze Johnson. A nigga that was heavy in the spotlight. A nigga that had graduated high school, went to college, and was recently drafted into the league.

"Do you hear yourself?" I frowned. "He a fucking square. Not no real street nigga. And this ain't even over no solid shit. This is all over a bitch. A bitch that wound up pregnant by you while she was engaged to another nigga. A rich nigga that she refuses to leave and probably didn't even tell she was pregnant. And if she did tell him, her scandalous ass probably got him thinking the baby is his."

Lawrence sucked his teeth at my comment. "I'm rich too nigga. Fuck is that supposed to mean?" his ignorant ass asked, disregarding everything else I'd said.

*I'm rich too.* What he meant was, *I* was rich. Lawrence had money but not ball player money like that nigga had. The bitch Casey that had him rattled, fired all up, and in his feelings over, dated rich niggas. She had just gotten caught up with his poor ass. He wasn't poor in the literal sense, but he was poor compared to Blaze that played for the fucking Atlanta Hawks.

"Whatever, Lawrence. Look, stay off that social media shit. All you gon' do is drive yourself crazy going back and forth with that nigga every time he say some fly shit. You can't do shit about it. You already on house arrest for chasing his ass down," I reminded him. "And now yo' hard-headed ass is still going back and forth with him. This corny ass shit done got public so if you send some steppers his way, all that shit is going to point and lead right back to you."

Just a few weeks ago, Lawrence was laid up over Casey house when Blaze came in unexpectedly acting a fool with his homies. Lawrence knew that Casey and Blaze were on and off, but he never expected him to stroll up in her crib like he ran shit. Bro was under the impression that she was was still his bitch. Lawrence being the hood nigga he was, flipped out, pistol-whipped and chased Blaze down with a big ass Glock 40. All that shit happened in an uppity-ass neighborhood, *on camera*. To make matters worse, even though it was "Casey's" house, the lease also had Blaze's name on it.

Despite the fact that Blaze was initially considered the aggressor, Lawrence was still in the wrong. Needless to say, he sat in jail for nearly a week while I tossed out nearly one-hundred thousand to get him out on bail. Despite having the money in abundance, I didn't like, nor was I about to keep kicking out bread for ridiculous and avoidable shit for Lawrence's fuck ass. Brother or not.

Lawrence and I had come from humble beginnings. I literally clawed and fought my way to the top, and when I finally made it, my own brother would become my biggest liability. Anybody that knew me, knew that he was the only nigga that could get away with outlandish shit. Anyone else would have been put right the fuck to sleep.

My brother continued fussing into the phone while I swiveled left and right in my office chair. Since it was a Monday, business was slow, and I had time to hide out and bullshit. The unexpected beep in my ear indicated that I had an incoming call.

"Bro, I'm gonna hit you back in a bit. I gotta call coming in I need to take."

The call wasn't really urgent. I was just no longer interested in hearing his rambling. Saved by the bell.

After hanging up with Lawrence, I clicked over to answer a call from a nigga name Boobie. He was a good dude that some-times surrounded himself with the wrong people; however, I still did business with him because he was capable of handling what I was supplying. Not everyone was.

"Wassup, Boobie?" I greeted him.

"Wassup, my nigga. I got a little situation I need to rap to you about."

I instantly noticed his voice was unusually serious. Boobie was a lively little nigga. Always chipper. Always laughing. The tone he'd just set on the phone was atypical.

"Aight nigga. I'll come holla at you 'bout it. Give me an hour and I'll pull up on you," I told him.

Boobie had a little body shop out Oakland City. I'd actually used him here and there to do minor work for me on vehicles I leased. Despite his shop being in the hood, he was actually very good at what he did. After agreeing to meet up, I hung up the phone and slid it across my desk. There wasn't much that I could do or say over the jack. That was law.

As one of the largest and quietest heroin dealers in the city, discretion was my strength. I had never been busted and never been caught up. I also owned a successful exotic and luxury car rental company. As far as the drugs, I worked directly with my brother and we were selective about who we dealt with as a whole. I was anyway. If I left it up to my brother Lawrence, he'd be selling to anyone, simply killing you if you crossed him. With my method, we only distributed drugs to about three other mid-level dealers and they, in turn, supplied most of the city. Lately, however, my plug had temporarily halted operations. Being the smart and patient nigga that I was, I too followed suit. I couldn't risk trying to get work from someone else. In grimy ass Atlanta, it was hard to determine what niggas were working with twelve and what niggas were jackboys. Money was never worth more than my freedom or my life. Even without an explanation, if he said it wasn't the time to move work, then that's what it was.

I'd met my connect, Luis, years back when I was still on a low scale of drug distribution. I had saved some money and was opening up my business: Luxe Car Collection. Luis had come in wanting to rent a whip while he was visiting Atlanta. I was impressed when he leased our most expensive car for an entire month. We began to chat and that's how our relationship began.

It seemed like just yesterday, but boy how blessed I was to meet him. That connection alone pushed me into millionaire status. I hadn't looked back since. To be honest, I didn't even need to sling dope. I only did it because Lawrence needed an avenue to make money. I figured it was better for me to continue running shit than to let him either get himself killed or let him end up killing a bunch of folks.

"So, this is what I'm paying you for?" I asked my younger sister, Lindsey, when I finally walked out of my office to inform her that I was about to head out for a few.

She was leaning up against the front of a shiny, black Bugatti, making faces, most likely posing for an Instagram picture.

"Stop! Don't mess up my shot," she whined while swatting away the hand I'd thrown in front of the iPhone camera in an attempt to photo bomb her. "Move," she demanded like I was the annoying one.

"Do some fuckin' work," I argued playfully.

"I am nigga. I'm trying to help yo' ugly self out. This is for the business Instagram page. It would be dry if it weren't for me. You need to do some advertising or something."

She got up off the Bugatti and came behind me.

"For what?" I asked with raised brows before stopping and turning around. "I'm not hurting for business. I sell out every weekend and I'm usually low on inventory during the weekday."

"Yeah, well low on inventory and *sold out* during the weekday is two different things," she countered with a smirk. "You always talking about opening another location, but you haven't done what's necessary to do so. You have the money. You just need the demand," she said, before walking ahead of me and sliding in the office chair behind the receptionist desk.

I walked to the front of the desk and smiled like a proud father. At eighteen years old, my sister was smart as fuck. Just a month ago, she'd graduated damn near at the top of her class at the expensive ass private school I'd put her in, and she basically ran my shit. She was all the help that I had and really needed.

Her problem was she didn't want to take on that role. She didn't want that responsibility of helping her big bro. She was like the typical young girl growing up in a morally corrupt city – hot in the ass and ready to run the streets like the bitches she was nothing like. Well maybe I was being a little dramatic.

Standing five-foot-seven and around one-hundred-fifteen pounds, Lindsey was considered skinny. No ass. No tits – just a beautiful face that reminded me of my own. She hated being rail thin in a world that glamorized and glorified big fake backsides and assets. Expresso skin, whiskey-colored irises, and long black hair, she was basically my younger twin. I was twenty-seven and had dreads while she bore thick, natural, shiny-black tresses that hung down her back. Even though my mama was wild back in the day, we all had the same daddy and thus looked alike. I was tall and thick while Lawrence was a tad shorter but similar in girth. Ladies loved us and Lawrence loved the ladies. I on the other hand didn't entertain too many of them. I struggled with demons that the average broad couldn't relate to.

Since I'd been on, every woman that I'd ran into had viewed me as a meal ticket. They thought that they could fuck me good and spend my bread up while they pretended to care about me. It didn't work like that. I was usually a good judge of character and when I did occasionally slip up, it didn't take me long to dissect and dismiss a bitch. My lifestyle didn't come easy and despite me trying to make it as easy as possible to maintain now that I was up, it wasn't. I didn't need or want a headache. Some loud-mouthed broad who'd rather argue than build. I wanted someone who provided me with peace. Someone who understood my former lifestyle and respected my current one. I didn't need a bitch calling me lame because I didn't want to turn up or party all night. Or one that preferred to shop all day spending my money but refused to help me run my business.

I wanted a woman, but I needed one that was strong, came from what I came from, and could relate to me on a deeper level. Someone who understood me. Unfortunately, that type of woman with class, was rare. Most of them were too far gone mentally. Broken down from the men they once loved or corrupted by a materialistic society that prided themselves on zero emotions for the opposite sex.

"And you also need to hire someone else," Lindsey stated firmly, reminding me that she no longer wanted to do things alone.

"You hire them. I got shit to do."

"So, Alexis really isn't coming back?" she asked softly, doing her best to be nosy, while appear caring.

I leaned up against the receptionist desk and got close to her so that she could see how serious I was.

"Absolutely not."

"She really pregnant?" she blurted out.

I immediately stood straight and stopped leaning against the desk. That was a subject that I definitely didn't want to go into. I knew Alexis probably told her that shit, which annoyed me since my sister had literally just turned eighteen and wasn't old enough to be in my business. Even if she was old enough, I still didn't want her in it.

"Can you stop worrying about Alexis and find someone please else to help out around her? Put out an ad and pick the best person or something. I gotta go take care of some business. I'll be back in an hour or two," I told her before walking out the front door of my business.

When I got into my pickup truck, I couldn't help but think about what my sister had just asked me about Alexis. Was she really pregnant? I prayed that her ass wasn't. She was the last bitch that I wanted to be stuck dealing with for eighteen entire years.

I'd met Alexis at a party one drunken night while I was out with Lawrence and a few others. I noticed her and her friends right away but for me, she stuck out the most. She was bad. Fat ass, pretty face, slim waist. To be honest, I actually preferred the natural look. But I was a sucker for a nice smile and a sense of humor. When she started talking, it was something about her bubbly personality and infectious smile that reeled me in. One thing led to another and it was on and popping. I wanted her and I made that crystal clear that night.

Her being so easy to get should have been a red flag; however, I wasn't really used to being told no so I didn't think too much of it. The thing was, I didn't approach broads that often; they usually approached me. Or they were doing some dumb shit to get noticed. For me, a big, beefy, handsome black nigga with shoulder-length dreads, being told no was a rare thing. I literally walked like money and talked like money. It wasn't like that was something I was trying to do. It was my aura. I wore simple shit. Basic shit like Ralph Lauren tees, and Diesel jeans. I wasn't walking around in no Amiri's. Labels weren't my thing. I didn't like wasting my money and I didn't need Gucci and Prada to let others know I was rich. I didn't care if a motherfucker knew if I was rich or not. But then again, it was the top-tier gold-digging bitches that knew that wealth was quiet. Not loud or flashy. Alexis was the bitch that knew. Even in a pair of jeans and a black Calvin Klein sweatshirt, she knew.

Needless to say, she fell right into position and played her cards exceptionally. Fucked me good. Sucked me good and pretended to be all for me. She was gorgeous, fun and I loved being around her. Within a month, I had her staying nights with me at my condo downtown, as well as helping my sister out at Luxe. I of course paid her to do that, on top of blessing her with the perks of being my main jawn. We weren't exclusive but I fucked with her heavy, so I only dealt with her. We weren't posting pictures together on social media, but I was spoiling her. Shopping sprees, getaways, entrance to exclusive-ass clubs and events. She had all that at her fingertips, but that hoe got comfortable and started changing.

Unfortunately, when a motherfucker was being fake, they could only keep up the charade for so long. I guess that was part of the game plan. Get a nigga hooked and try to weaken him.

The thing was, I wasn't a weak nigga. I was a *real* nigga. I quickly realized the hoe didn't want to do shit. All of a sudden, helping out at Luxe became beneath her. Going out three times a week with her girlfriends was the norm, and me not participating made me lame. Every other day she was starting an argument about her not being happy. Or me being boring. It was always something.

Me being the nigga that I was, I tried to satisfy her. I was a hood nigga, yeah, but I was also a man. A man that fucked with shawty and was trying to make shit work. The final straw was when I walked in on her sniffing coke in the bathroom of my crib. I couldn't help but be turned off and done. I literally scooped that bitch up by her bundles, put her out my spot, and tossed her back to where she so desperately wanted to be: the motherfucking streets! Since then, I had been alone. I fucked a little shawty every now and then, but nothing was serious. I needed a certain type of woman and until I found it, I was straight. I didn't even miss Alexis or nothing. When I fucked with someone, I fucked with them wholeheartedly. When I stopped fucking with someone, the same shit applied.

Meanwhile, Alexis was blowing me up and crying to anyone that would listen about how I supposedly had done *her*. Cutting her off financially and firing her from a job that she said she didn't want. Now, she was supposed to be pregnant and was saying it was mine. If she wasn't calling my business, she was calling my sister, or my mama. Shawty had become a mean ass headache. Lawrence wasn't the only nigga that had a situation. I did as well. The difference for me and him was that I didn't want Alexis' ass or any baby that she was claiming to be carrying. I knew what I was saying was harsh, but it was the truth. After shaking coke-sniffing Alexis from my thoughts, I hopped on the road and headed to see what the fuck was up with Boobie.

After driving for about ten minutes, I finally got to Oakland City and made my way into Boobie's shop. When I walked to the back and entered his office, I found him seated behind his little desk on a call. As soon as he saw me, he wrapped it right up, and got straight to what was going on. It didn't take long for my blood to start running hot.

I let him talk and didn't say much. When I dealt with men, I always kept my cool and never let a nigga know what I was thinking or feeling. I wasn't saying much but I was seething. He couldn't tell though. It was shit like what he just told me that had me ready to break Lawrence's fucking neck. At times, I wondered if he intentionally defied me. Like he thought I was soft or something because we were no longer in the trenches. Or maybe it was because he was my flesh and blood and felt like he automatically received a pass or something.

Boobie had basically told me that even though I had stopped supplying Lawrence with work to distribute amongst the three niggas we normally dealt with, he had gone behind my back and continued supplying them with some shit from only who fucking knew.

To make matters worse, the shit that he had given them had addicts overdosing and dropping like flies. The drugs had been so heavily cut with the synthetic opioid Fentanyl, that it was killing motherfuckers in large numbers.

"A nigga ain't think to even run it by you or nothing," Boobie continued to explain. "We always worked with him, and since day one, for the most part, he been the one always handling shit."

"Right. Right." I nodded in agreement.

I definitely wasn't putting any type of blame on him. Lawrence was guilty of all charges. "I know you ain't know ... But now that you do."

I paused. I didn't even have to finish the sentence. Boobie nodded and raised his hands up. "I know. Don't accept anything else from him until you okay it."

"Actually, you won't be accepting anything else from him at all. When I'm back in motion, I'll give you the details."

I was seriously contemplating saying fuck the drug game as a whole. I didn't need the money. I had only been orchestrating and financing the shit because with my connect it was easy and it helped my brother Lawrence feel like he had a purpose. Lawrence was a modern-day Mitch from Paid in Full. He loved the game and loved all the so-called glitz and glam that came with it. After I made my statement, Boobie paused for a few seconds. I could tell that he wanted to say something, but he was hesitating.

"You gotta question or something?" If so, I wanted the nigga to spit it the fuck out.

"Actually, I do. Look, the niggas that I deal to and the niggas that they deal to, can't afford to sit without product for weeks, let alone months. They're either gonna find a new supplier ... or."

"You'll have to find a new supplier," I finished his sentence for him. He nodded.

I, in turn stood there quietly and peered at Boobie for a second. A few seconds later, I softened my stern expression and smirked.

"Good luck with that. As you can see from the bullshit you just got, quality is an issue, and you and I both know that quality has never been an issue for me."

I didn't mean for it to come out arrogant. Facts were facts. The nigga could do what the fuck he wanted but as long as my plug was at a standstill then he was going to have problems getting work that compared. Not only that, he was going to have to deal with scorching hot streets because the police were damn sure going to be on niggas asses to see who was selling all the fucked-up dope that had folks dying left and right.

"Look, I can't tell you what to do. Do what's best for you and your team. Frankly, I prefer to be fair rather than selfish. I want to see a man get money, but as long as my plug isn't moving, neither am I. I'll see if Lawrence takes that shit back so you and ya people don't suffer to big a loss... but I doubt it. He isn't as fair as I am, and everyone knows that."

Just as Boobie went to speak, a slim, brown-skinned nigga

with thick spongy hair walked in. He was a clean, square-looking cat. I'd seen him around a few times, but I didn't know him or know too much about him.

"Wassup." He nodded his head at me as greeting and then turned to Boobie.

"The nigga Cuddy outside. He knows you busy but he tryin' to get an update."

Boobie's expression immediately hardened.

"Nothing's changed. That nigga knows that and so do you. And when I'm busy, you're second in charge, so why can't you tell that nigga what you already know?" he asked irritably.

"Lance, this is my cousin Neal. Neal, this is Lance."

Just as he went to reply, a pretty, but angry-looking broad pushed through the door. As soon as she opened her mouth, I knew that our conversation was over and she was about to be the one doing all the talking.

## ❧ 4 ❧

## ALIZE

I was so many things at once: frustrated, angry, and scared. I
had no place to stay and the little bit of funds I had were
dwindling rapidly by the day. Hearing Neal basically say
fuck me and our girls over the phone sent me into a rage. After
flying back in from Vegas and arriving back at Aunt Melva's, I
didn't waste any time packing my belongings.

Even though I'd told her on the phone that I was going to
pay her, I never had any intention of doing so. Not after the
dumb shit she demanded over the phone. I simply agreed
because I didn't want to have to kill her for mistreating my girls
over money. Since she wanted to be greedy, I didn't give her ass
one fuckin' cent. I instead gathered my shit, packed up my girls
in my Hyundai and rolled.

I could admit that I was scared and I didn't know what the
fuck I was doing or where the fuck we were going. I'd called
around to almost a dozen hotels and everyone had given me
monthly rates that would have left me flat broke. Once again, I
called Neal to see if he could help, and he refused. The whole
time he talked shit, I felt myself getting angrier by the minute.
The whole time he talked his shit, I was doing my best to figure
out where he was so I could run down on him. He didn't seem to

notice but I had always been observant. Running the streets with my mother taught me early about the importance of paying attention. I watched my surroundings and I also listened. When Neal was talking shit on the phone, I could hear the clunking and clanking sounds of metal in the background. I could also hear the distinct sound of an air impact wrench in the back. I instantly knew he was at Boobie's body shop. I wasted no time racing over there after he hung up on me

I didn't care what anybody thought or said. I knew I had said that I wasn't asking him for shit else, but my situation had changed. He was going to take care of his motherfucking kids or I was going to show my natural black fuckin' ass. He had the means to support us in many ways. All I wanted was a hotel room paid up for a few weeks. He was going to do right, or I was going to do his ass dirty. It was his choice. He had the right one that day. Like I said before, I let a lot slide when it came to how people treated me, but I was gon' step about my motherfucking kids. That's what a mother did.

I pulled up to Boobie's shop about fifteen-minutes after getting off the phone with Neal. I hadn't calmed down a bit. Nope. I was still fuming. Heat literally traveling through my body. Palms sweating. Heart racing. Ready to show off. Putting my car in park, and killing the engine, I instructed my girls to get out. I hit my fob and locked my door and then proceeded to storm up in Boobie's shop.

It was a small shop. He had about four bays with a large garage like building attached. Neal didn't know shit about cars, so I knew he wasn't in one of the bays. The main building was nearly empty inside except for a worker named Cuddy standing around, probably waiting to pick up a package. I'd seen him around a few times and didn't have anything against him. However, because of my attitude that day, I didn't acknowledge him when he tried to speak. All I could focus on was finding Neal's bum ass. I was heading straight to the back where Boobie's little corner office was located. I knew he would probably be there. Boobie didn't have folks lingering around too long. They came for whatever they came for and kept it moving.

After ignoring Cuddy's 'Wassup Alize,' he dashed behind me in an attempt to stop me. I guess he had gotten a glimpse of my angry face and realized I hadn't come with shits and giggles.

"Yo, Alize, they back there handling some shit," he called out. "I wouldn't go in there."

He was too late though. I was already at the door, turning the knob and walking through it. I immediately came face-to-face with an angry *and* an embarrassed-looking Neal. I didn't give a fuck though. The pussy didn't care how I felt when he talked shit or constantly hung the phone up in my ear.

"I knew yo' bitch ass was here!" I fussed angrily while I waved my hand in the air like I wanted all the smoke. "Like the fuck I was saying on the phone before you hung up on me, I need money for your girls!"

I stared Neal directly in his face with an angry scowl. I wasn't about to keep playing with him. He wasn't the only one who could act dumb. I noticed Boobie shaking his head in displeasure, while I also noticed another guy standing in the corner, doing his best to mind his business. My eyes met his and lingered for a moment. I couldn't help but notice he was black and fine as a motherfucker, but I hadn't come there to admire niggas. I rolled my eyes and made a 'what nigga" face, before turning my attention back to Neal.

"Alize, yo this not the place for –"

"Fuck you, Boobie!" I spat, cutting him off. "You ain't shit either! Don't tell me what is and ain't the place when it comes to my girls!"

I didn't want to hear shit from him either. He knew how Neal was, and he also knew me personally and knew our situation. He knew damn well that I had been put out of my apartment and was struggling with that nigga kids. I couldn't stand a bunch of so-called, "getting money" niggas that were too pussy to say, 'take care of your babies.'

"Yo, chill the fuck out! We can go outside and talk!" Neal argued, face flushed with embarrassment since I'd shamed in in front of the nigga that he worked for. Cousin or no cousin, it wasn't a good look.

"Pussy, you didn't want to talk when I tried. You hung up on me. And there isn't shit to talk about. I asked you for money! I still need that money! So, is you gon' give me that fuckin' money! Plain and simple! You run around all day living yo' best fuckin' life while I struggle with your girls!"

I could feel eyes burning through me, so I spun my head around to Boobie, and the other nigga in the room. I didn't usually like folks in my business, but I wanted to prove a point of how lame Neal's ass was. Boobie was still shaking his head in embarrassment while the black nigga stood there smirking like he was amused by the entire ghetto fiasco.

"My living situation is all fucked up. I have his two kids as you can see. This nigga got a pocket-full of money and won't don't shit for us! Help me make it make sense!" I argued.

"Who fault is that though?" he asked, before walking up to me, grabbing my free arm and pulling me out of the office with the girls.

I guess he'd had enough of me airing out his dirty laundry in front of niggas. When we got outside, the door to the office closed and I snatched away from Neal.

"Why the fuck you come up in a nigga business doing this shit?" he demanded to know.

"Fuck Bobbie and his business!" I spat. "You think I give a fuck about that when your girls need a place to stay! He don't give a fuck about us and neither do you! We have nowhere to go Neal! Nowhere! Aunt Melva put us out and I have to stay in a motel. I barely have enough money to last a week in a room. Soon, I'll be in my fuckin' car with your kids, Neal! They're your fuckin' kids!" I reminded him furiously.

At that moment, something in me broke and the emotions began pouring out. I was just sick and fucking tired. Of everything and everyone. I broke down. My voice cracked and I began sobbing.

"They're *your kids,* Neal. I shouldn't have to want to be with you for you to do right by your kids. You won't help me out of spite, and you know that's all it is. You want me to take them to a homeless shelter?" I cried.

Maybe it was me. Maybe I was the delusional one. But the nigga was being seriously unreasonable. A real man wouldn't see his children out on the street.

Neal's face softened and I could tell that he knew what he was doing was wrong. He walked towards me and tried to throw his arms around me to embrace me, but I snatched back.

"I don't need your sympathy," I spat coldly, despite the tears still running. "I need money!"

"How much do you need?" he asked me, before crouching down on one knee and finally greeting the girls. Unlike me, they gladly accepted his embrace. When he stood back up, he repeated the question.

"How much do you need Alize?" he asked, while I continued to sob quietly.

"Like a grand," I replied.

"Okay." He nodded. "And what does this grand cover?"

"A hotel room for a month. It's not the best room or the best area, but I'll make it work. At this point, I don't care where it is. As long as I have somewhere to take my kids."

Neal reached into his pocket and pulled out a knot. He carefully peeled ten, one-hundred-dollar bills away from it.

"Here." He handed me the money like it was nothing. I grabbed it quickly and stuffed it into my purse.

"Come on girls," I said.

"So, no thank you?" He glared at me and shook his head in disbelief.

"Thank you for what? You did what you were supposed to do," I said. I used the back of my hand to swipe the tears away from my face.

"Girls, say bye to your Daddy."

Neal shook his head dejectedly before leaning back down and quickly hugging the girls. They said goodbye and I headed back out the same way I'd stormed in.

\*\*\*

The girls and I were staying at an extended stay motel, similar to Intown suites. It wasn't much, but we had our own bathroom, our own little couch and table, as well as a small kitchenette, so I was able to prepare hot meals. The little space provided us with some privacy, so we didn't feel as homeless as we really were. To say I was stressed was a huge understatement. My life had changed overnight. The life I had provided for my girls had changed overnight. Living in the hood hadn't never been much, but I prided myself on giving them something that I'd never had, and that was stability. It was something that I had taken for granted and desperately wanted back. Despite battling my internal feelings that felt damn near like depression, I did my best to display a happy face and positive spirit for Sage and Violet.

"Girls, it's time for bed," I said.

They had been sitting on the floor, eyes glued to the little twenty-six-inch television. They had already been fed and bathed, and since it was nearing nine at night, it was time for them to lay it down. I took both of them by their hand, helping them hop up off the floor so they could climb up into the nearby bed. It was time to sit with them and go over our nightly talk. I had been having the same talk with them since we moved into the motel a few weeks backs.

"Sage, tell Mommy what we are doing tonight. Can you repeat to me what we've been going over since I started work?"

Sage nodded her head vigorously and looked at me with the sweetest smile before speaking. I already knew that she would be able to recite everything to me, but I needed to hear it from her mouth every night as confirmation. It was something that I had to drill into their heads because I needed them to know how important it was to listen and follow what I told them.

"You're going to work and we're going to bed."

"And what does that mean you can and cannot do?" I asked, the look on my face urging her to continue.

"We have to stay in bed. We can't watch TV, and we can't open the door for anybody, no matter who it is."

"Exactly, Sage. Good job. Where does Mommy work at, Violet?"

I turned my questioning to my younger daughter. I wanted to make sure she too could comprehend the rules.

"Walmart," she replied happily.

"Right. Mommy will be at work while you girls sleep, and I'll be home before you wake."

I pointed to their little personal cell phone that I had propped up on a chair right beside the bed.

"Who is that phone for?" I asked.

"You," the girls said in unison.

"And who can you two call on that phone?" I eyed them curiously.

"No one."

"Right. That phone is so I can see you two while I work. So, even though Mommy isn't in the same room, I'm still with you, watching you. So, good job girls."

I tapped both their butts so they could go on and lay down. I was all done with my twenty-one questions. I quickly tucked them in and then called their phone via FaceTime. That phone was my lifeline. It was my connection to my girls while I was away. It was like a baby monitor for me.

After kissing the both of them good night and turning every light switch off except the bathroom, I headed out to my overnight job, stocking at Walmart. I always had a sick feeling when I pulled out of the parking lot of the motel. For one, the motel itself wasn't in the best of locations. The monthly rate was less than nine hundred per month, making it affordable and accessible for drug addicts and prostitutes to come and go. Second, Sage and Violet were simply too young to be left alone. I hated leaving them. I felt like a failure and a bad mother. I hated saying 'I had to do what I had to do', but I did. I didn't have any help.

After acting a fool to get that little grand from Neal, he had text me and told me not to ask him for anything else. *Take me up for child support*, were his words. That was some stupid shit a spiteful nigga would say. I was definitely going to make good on that child-support request. In the meantime, I had to make some money so I could get out of the motel and get up in a spot.

I had come to the firm conclusion that nobody was helping me with anything. All I had were my girls and all they had was me. I didn't have time for a pity party. My main priority was to stack a little more money so I could pay a security deposit and first month's rent on a place. Once that was done, I was going to go back to school or something. Walmart was cool, but it wasn't enough for me to provide my girls with a better life.

Since my job wasn't far, I arrived at work in eight minutes. I locked up my Hyundai and clocked in to begin my shift. As usual, the time began flying by. At Walmart, we got breaks every two hours, so every two hours, I would peek in on my girls via the FaceTime call that I kept going all night. During my hour lunch break, I dashed back to the motel and slipped into the room to ensure they were asleep, before heading back to the store.

My whole little nightly work routine was illegal as fuck, but it was what it was. I'd attempted to enroll them into daycare but it simply wasn't practical. For two children it came to nearly three-hundred per week. I only made four hundred per week, working at Walmart. I'd even tried applying for assistance through the state to help with childcare, but I'd gotten thrown on the waiting list. There was no telling when I'd come off. I didn't bother asking Neal to watch his own kids because I knew he would find every excuse in the book not to. I also didn't want to hip him to the fact that I was leaving them alone at night by themselves. He had told me to take them to his mother, and I had tried, but she also worked nights and our schedules overlapped by several hours. Since I barely had a dime to my name, I wasn't able be particularly picky about what I would and wouldn't accept jobwise. When Walmart called me, I took it without thinking.

I returned to work and as expected, the night flew by. That was a good thing, because while my job stocking was easy, working the overnight shift as a whole was tough. Since it was summertime, my girls weren't in school. Violet and Sage were slated to go to Pre-K and Kindergarten, respectively in the fall. Until then, I was up with them, instead of sleeping. I arrived home around ten after six. After getting settled, taking a quick shower and laying down, I only wound up getting a few hours asleep before the girls were right back up. Luckily, they were well behaved for the most part so I knew I would be able to eventually lay back down.

The girls wound up getting up around nine, which was their regular time. I made them a light breakfast of oatmeal and sausage and then turned on the TV so they could watch cartoons and I could go back to sleep for a few more hours.

When I finally woke back up, it was damn near twelve in the afternoon, and they were asking me to take them to get ice cream. They weren't asking for much, so I hopped up, got myself together, and we headed out.

The motel that we stayed at wasn't very large, meaning there weren't a ton of parking spots outside. So, I was highly confused when we walked outside to get in the car, but I didn't see it parked where I remembered parking it. After pacing the parking lot and checking the other side of the property, I realized that it wasn't there. Which didn't make any fucking sense! My car was paid for, so I wasn't concerned that it had been repossessed. However, Neal had definitely purchased it, so I figured snatching up my car was one of his spiteful attempts to get back at me.

"Mommy, where's the car?" Violet whined.

I dug into my purse and pulled my phone out so I could call Neal.

"Neal, did you take my car?" I asked angrily.

"What? Yo, why every time you call me it's on some bullshit or some fucking drama," he complained, sounding truly irritated by my call.

"Did you take my fucking car or not? I'm staying at this shitty, raggedy ass hotel with your fucking kids and now all of a sudden, my fucking car is gone. I need my shit to get back and forth to work. And I also need it to transport around your fucking kids. I know you fuckin' have it!" I argued. While I waited for him to respond, I searched the parking lot one more time.

"Yo, do you hear yourself? You just said you're at a shitty ass hotel in what I assume to be a bullshit neighborhood ... even though I told you that you could take the girls to my mother. Let's not forget I gave you a thousand dollars and that's the bull-shit you picked. But of course, Alize gotta do everything her own selfish ass way. It's fuckin' Atlanta Einstein! Somebody prob-ably stole it. I know I didn't take it. The fuck would I want with it?"

"Why the fuck would someone steal a Hyundai?"

"I don't fucking know. Maybe because it's a common-ass, basic-ass car and they could bust it down for parts. All I know is, I don't have your fucking shit. Now stop calling me with the dumb shit," he said angrily before banging the phone in my ear.

"Mommy, are we still going to get ice cream?" Violet asked, her syrupy voice instantly soothing me. I took a deep breath before replying. I had to do better. Children picked up on energy and my energy had been way off for far too long.

"I'm so sorry girls. I don't think that ice cream's happening," I admitted to them. "Mommy's car is gone."

"Someone stole it?" Sage asked, her eyes widening.

"I think so sweetie. I'm going to have to call the police."

I hated calling twelve, but in that situation, I had no choice. "Fuck," I mumbled quietly. I hated fuckin' Atlanta.

A week passed and I still had no car. Since the Hyundai was paid for, I only had liability car insurance on it. Without comprehensive coverage, I couldn't even file a claim. All I could do was hope and pray that my shit was eventually found and that it hadn't been chopped down for parts.

At that point, I no longer believed in luck. I had been tested on so many levels. With my car gone, everything had become two times harder. I didn't work far but getting to work was still becoming expensive. I had to take an Uber to and from Walmart which was nearly one-hundred dollars a week. It wasn't much to some, but for a single mom on a budget, living in a motel room, it was a lot. I also couldn't drop in on my girls nightly and check on them, which I absolutely hated. It was like something or somebody was trying to break me. I couldn't understand it. I couldn't understand what I'd done to have such bad luck.

Not one to cry over spilled milk, I kept it pushing and prepared myself for work. I had already gone over the same little question and answering session with my girls and headed out. As soon as I walked out the door of my room and stepped outside, something in my head told me to stay home. It was a wet mess outside. It was literally pouring down raining with thick, fat clouds covering the sky. The rain was so heavy it sounded like it was pounding down on the vehicles in the parking lot. It had been raining all day and it didn't seem to be slowing up. Before I'd left the room, I'd checked my phone and the weatherman had called for severe thunderstorms. Before I had even left, I could hear the rumbling thunder along with the whipping and cracking sounds ripping through the sky. The way it was coming down, I knew there would soon be lightning following it.

I wasn't thinking about staying in the house because I was

scared of a little rain; the problem for me was that my cell phone service had been shotty and so had the girl's phone. Before I left, I had to set up the girl's phone twice since the calls kept dropping. Within a ten-minute period, our FaceTime call had dropped twice. Instead of calling out, I decided to still go ahead and continue into work.

I caught my Uber and started my night off as I usually did. Since it was still raining, I kept checking on my girls. At first the calls were freezing and eventually they started dropping again. I wasn't surprised since it was still pouring outside and like I expected, there had been reported lightning. Even the lights at Walmart had flickered a few times.

*Fuck this shit*, I thought. I wasn't feeling the fact that I couldn't reach them, and I knew that all that loud ass thunder was going to have them scared. I didn't want to keep calling and calling, because then they would never get to sleep. I decided that I was going to finish stocking the last few boxes on my cart and then let my boss know that I had to leave early. My kids were more important. Nothing was more important than them, especially not no damn job. I figured it wouldn't be an issue though, since I never called out and I had only been late once since I'd been working there. Even if it were an issue, I was still leaving.

About an hour later, I finished loading up the last box of eggs and was ready to let my boss know I was out. I stopped in my tracks when I noticed that my boss was already headed towards me, but he had two uniformed police officers with him. For some reason, I just knew they were headed to me. I just knew that something had happened.

"There she is," my manager Tim said before shooting me a look of concern and walking off.

"Ma'am. Are you Alize McKoy?" he asked.

"Yes, I am," I stammered out, damn near choking in fear. It was something about the serious looks on their face and the fact that they wore police uniforms that had me shook. I knew it had something to do with my girls.

"Well, I'm Officer Diez and this is Officer Noland with the Atlanta Police Department. Ma'am, your children called 911 indicating that they were in danger. I'm sure they were just frightened because of the storm. But when the dispatcher asked if there was anyone with them, they told her no. We were dispatched out to the location and after advising front desk that we had suspicion of unaccompanied minors, we were allowed access to the room. Your kids were scared, but they're safe. Unfortunately, ma'am, that means that we're going to have to take you into custody."

I covered my mouth with the palm of my hand and squeezed my eyes shut. There was nothing that I could say. Nothing that I could do to defend myself. When I reopened my eyes, one of the officers, the older looking one of the two, shot me a disapproving look, while the other gave me a look of sympathy. I didn't care about their judgment. All I cared about were my children.

I suddenly felt my chest was deflating. It was like all the air and all the life has been sucked from my body. I couldn't fucking win no matter how hard I fucking tried! I had suffered so much. Since I was a kid. Now, I was hit with the biggest blow I'd ever had in my life. It was bigger than being taken from my mother. Bigger than losing my mom at twelve-years-old after she had been beat to death by another addict she was trying to steal a ten-dollar bag from.

Them telling me that they had to take me into custody didn't mean shit to me. The biggest blow came from knowing that they were about to take my fucking kids.

"Wh-Where are my kids?" I stammered.

I couldn't hold back the tears. They began pouring down my face as I was immediately overcome with guilt, sadness, and regret. I was angry because like so many others, I was trying and still losing. The biggest feeling was disappointment. I was disappointed in myself for failing my children. Disappointed for being naive and constantly believing people when they said they had my back. I so desperately wanted to stand on my own, but I was failing.

"Ma'am, your girls are safe in another squad car, but unfortunately, we won't be able to release them back to you. You're gonna have to call someone that can come and get them. Someone who they will be safe with. If there is no one to call, then we will have to place them in custody of the state. Unfortunately, that is the procedure that we have to follow."

With vacant eyes, I nodded my head, acknowledging the fact that I understood. While I continued to stand there and sob, the cop that had initially given me the disapproving look began to speak.

"Ma'am, we're going to have to ask you to turn around. I'm going to go ahead and read you your rights."

I didn't even bother asking him if they could cuff me outside. I didn't give a fuck about none of the customers at Walmart, and I didn't give a fuck about none of the employees either. All I cared about were my kids and how they were being taken from me. Other than that, I didn't give a fuck about much else. I wasn't perfect and I knew it. Was I prideful – Yes! Was I wrong for leaving my girls alone in that motel by themselves – absolutely! But was I a horrible mother because I did what I did to provide for my girls? I didn't think so. It didn't matter what I thought though. I was going to take whatever they gave me because I had no choice but to be accountable.

I turned around and the officer took my wrists and placed my limp hands behind my back. I was cuffed, taken into custody, and booked at the city jail on child neglect and endangerment charges.

Sitting in the city jail was the lowest I had ever felt. It was the weakest I had ever been. It was a turning point for me. I had to do something different. Hearing them say that I wasn't going to get my kids back right away was like a knife in my heart. It was like losing my breath and never catching it again. I was at a loss for words. Just lost period. Empty.

Sage and Violet were everything to me. I wasn't sure how things were going to play out, but I knew that I was going to fight to get my children back. I wasn't Niecy. I was Alize. I refused to lose my girls and not get them back. I refused to let my kids go into a home where they weren't loved. A place where they were only viewed as a paycheck. Hell nah. I was going to fight for mine.

⚜

Neal and his mother Judy ended up picking the girls up from the police station before child services could get there. Even though he and I still weren't on the best of terms, Neal assured me that I wouldn't spend a night in jail. I had no doubt that Judy had a lot to do with that. She and I had always had a good relationship. She knew I wasn't a bad mother.

Even though I was on a tiny, uncomfortable, metal cot, I was still able to get a little sleep because I knew that my girls were safe and were somewhere with someone that actually loved them. In the morning when I woke up, I got a bond. They allowed me one phone call, so I called Judy to let her know what my bond was. She of course said that she would inform her son.

A few hours later, Neal made good on his promise and posted my bail. He even brought his raggedy ass to the jail and picked me up. After the release process, I damn near ran out the front door of the city jail. I had never appreciated air so much until then. I raced to the parking spot where Neal was parked in his lime-green Dodge Charger waiting for me. I was hoping that he'd brought the girls with him, but I was instantly met with disappointment when I opened the car door and didn't see anyone but him. Considering the fact that he had just post my bond, I wasn't going to be ungrateful by climbing in his whip talking shit.

"You okay Ms. Independent?" he asked sarcastically as soon as I dropped down and settled comfortably into his car seat. It was typical of his nappy-headed ass to try and make jokes at a time like that.

I sighed before leaning up and adjusting the vent so the cool air could blast directly into my face. It was hot and I didn't want to argue.

"I'm good, Neal. Thanks for asking, even though you trying to be smart." I rolled my eyes and looked straight ahead. "I appreciate you coming to get me. You didn't have to, but you did, and I thank you."

"Wasn't about shit, shawty. And you know my mama wasn't having you sitting up in jail over no bullshit bond." He laughed. "You know me. I was gon' let yo' ass sit in that bitch about forty-eight hours to teach you a lesson."

He chuckled lightly as he looked over at me, but I rolled my eyes silently again and looked out the window.

"Why didn't you ask for help?"

That, of course, immediately pissed me off. I turned my head and eyed him with a questioning look.

"You know damn well that I been asking you for help. You gave me the thousand dollars and then you gave me yo' ass to kiss, so please do not sit here and act like all this shit that's happening is solely my fucking fault. It takes a village to raise children, and I didn't even have a piece of one. In order to work, I need daycare. A fuckin' vehicle. I didn't have none of that shit. You knew exactly what I was up against and you knew what I was going through, but you wanted me to go through it because you wanted me to need you," I argued.

"Oh, so now this is all my fault? You can't put all that shit on me, Alize. You left me, remember? And I told you that you could take the kids to my mom. You know when she available. Ain't nobody tell you to go and get a job overnight when you know she works until after midnight at the hospital."

We had been sitting idle in Neal's Charger, but he finally put it in drive and started pulling away from the city jail.

"You hungry?"

"No. Just take me back to my motel room," I demanded, clearly annoyed.

"Now you got an attitude? After a nigga just bonded yo' ass out of jail. Un-fucking believable," he scoffed.

"How many times do you want me to say thank you, Neal? I said it once and I'm not gonna say it again. And you know that I'm not trying to put shit on you but please don't sit here and act like I'm a piece of shit mother because I'm not. Please don't act like I didn't ask you for help."

I angrily folded my arms into my chest.

"Like I just wanted to leave my kids by themselves to go out and fuck and party or something," I continued to argue. "I wasn't doing none of that shit. I was working! Doing what I thought was best for them, and I fucked up. I need a place, Neal. I can't be in a fucking motel with your girls," I argued.

I fought back the urge to cry again but I quickly shook it off. That shit wasn't getting me nowhere. I thought about what Melvina had said and she was right. I had a lot of pride and it was flaw. I had a nigga in front of me with the cash I needed. It was time to start playing my cards right. Neal was doing me the way he was because I wasn't fucking with him. He wanted me. I didn't want him. Didn't that technically mean that I had the upper hand? I was about to see.

Neal glanced at me while I sat in the seat, lip trembling, my raw emotions on full display.

"What the fuck do you want from me, Neal? You want me to suffer? Because if I'm suffering, then so are your girls."

Neal sat there quietly for a minute. He sighed, glanced over at me and then finally spoke.

"You know I don't want to see you or my girls suffer. But I ain't gon' lie like a nigga don't want you back. I don't like how you been carrying me though. Ignoring me, cursing me out, embarrassing me. I'm a man at the end of the day."

*Hardly.* I damn near blurted those thoughts out.

"I fucked up by fucking Melissa. But do I want her? Hell no. Do I love her? Of course not. But I love you, and I want you back."

I could have spit in Neal's face. He didn't love shit but money and himself. I had to question his love for his daughters at times. But I was gon' tell his ass what he wanted to hear. For the moment anyway.

"You know I love you too, Neal." That part wasn't a lie. "I need time though. I need for us to be away from each other for a while. I need you to help me get into a new place." That was really all I cared about. I didn't give a fuck about a car or anything. I would Uber my way through Atlanta. I needed a spot so I could get the girls back.

"Okay." He nodded. "I'll help you get into a place. I'll help you with whatever you need. If that means that we working on us. That we gon' work shit out and that I'm gonna be coming in with you when you find something."

"I agree to that," I lied. It would be a cold day in Hell before I took his ass back.

"When is the rent on the room due?" he asked.

"In about a week."

"I gotchu. Go ahead and run me the address. When I drop you off, I'll pay it up for a month or two. That'll give you time to start looking for something. And I want you to start looking asap," he instructed.

It was funny how all of a sudden, he was so eager to help. All of a sudden, he wanted me to get into a place right away. The nigga just wanted to have his cake and eat it too. But I was going to play along. My way wasn't working. I had to do shit differently if I wanted to get back right for my girls. I didn't even bother asking about another car. I would take care of that on my own. With him paying my rent up, I was going to continue stacking my bread. There was no way that I was going back up into Walmart after getting arrested there. I was going to start looking for a new job as soon as I got back to my room. Either way, Neal was going to help me get the ball rolling. This time though, we weren't playing in his field; we were playing in mine.

## 5

# LANCE


I was sitting at my desk, pushing my dreads out my face and rubbing my temples when I heard the door open. I looked up. It was Lindsey, peeking her head in.

"You okay?" she asked gently.

She had just transferred a call from Alexis to my desk and the short conversation that we had instantly made my brain pound against my fucking skull. It was always the same shit. 'We need to work things out because I'm having your baby.' Nothing that I wanted to hear. When I expressed that to her, she'd get mad and curse me out all kinds of ways. Frankly, the shit was getting old.

"Yeah, I'm good. Do me a favor though, block shawty. I already got her blocked on my phone but all that calling up here shit, gotta stop. I swear I be ready to just pay somebody to beat her fucking ass." I knew a couple bitches from the hood that would tune her ass up for a blunt and a pint of Henny.

"Okay. I'll figure out how to block her number and call the phone company. But—"

"But what, Lindsey?" I sighed. I stopped rubbing my head and looked up at her.

"Don't get no attitude with me nigga. You picked her," she joked.

I glared at her. I didn't find shit funny at all. Alexis' ass was getting on my damn nerves and so was she. She joked and played too much when a nigga was being serious.

"No for real though. You gonna have to find a way to deal with her, because even if I block her, she still can just keep calling from a different number. So, it's pointless," she added in a childish tone. "But! I just hired someone, and I would like for you to cheer up and come out and meet her. I'm ready to get her trained so I can get out of this childish environment and roll out for the summer."

"Okay," I replied, ignoring the smart shit she had said. "You can get out now," I said, her big ass head still poking through the door.

She flashed a smile and then stuck her middle finger up at me as she closed the door. I shook my head but couldn't help but chuckle. Lindsey got on my damn nerves but that was my baby for real. She could get anything she wanted from me, even after doing the dumb shit.

I got up my desk and headed out to the front where my new hire was standing. As I rounded the corner and got to the front of the door, I was met with a familiar face.

"Lance, this is Alize. Your new hire."

She turned to Alize. "Alize, this is Lance, my brother, the owner, *and* your new boss."

She flashed a big, fake ass smile which caused me to grin on some silly shit as well. Judging by the grin, she remembered me just like I'd remembered her.

"Nice to meet you, Lance," she said, extending her hand so I could shake it. I took it and held it for a minute, briefly admiring how soft and smooth it felt against my own. Feeling myself unintentionally stiffen, I released her hand and studied her.

"Likewise, Alize. But let's be honest. We've met before."

The last time I'd seen Alize, she was angry and going off; however, as she stood in front of me today, she was calm and it allowed me to take in all of her beauty. Every single drop. She didn't have a stitch of makeup on. Just some lip gloss coating her thick, juicy lips and probably some mascara because I could low-key see that shit clumping up. Despite all that, she was cute as fuck. Highly appealing.

"You got that. We have met, and thankfully, I'm hired already. Please, let's forget that day." She laughed nervously, pushing a strand of hair away from her face.

Peeping the awkward reunion, Lindsey stood there and eyed us curiously. "You two met before?" She looked at Alize and turned her head to me.

"Something like that."

I looked at my nosy ass sister and asked, "When is she starting?"

I honestly didn't give a fuck about how she had gone off on her baby daddy at the body shop. That nigga probably deserved it. Besides, I was drawn to her, and it was so much deeper than the simple fact that she was pretty and lively. I'd recognized shawty in more ways than one. When I'd seen her at the shop, I knew she looked familiar. But seeing her standing in my business that day, I instantly realized where I *really* knew her from. She had that same rich brown skin and deep-set eyes as her mother. She was Niecy's daughter.

The same Niecy that Black had told Cj to piss on in the alleyway years ago when we were kids. It was also the same Black that tried some similar shit like that with my own drug-addicted mama, but I smoked his ass before he could pull his dick out.

Seeing Alize not only brought back feelings of nostalgia, it also brought back past regrets and demons that I'd been strug-gling with since I was sixteen. I was a firm believer of fate, but I wasn't going to speak to soon. I wanted to sit down with her. Chat a little. Then I would know.

Although, I knew she had some drama going on, Alize had grown up to be beautiful. Yeah, she was a zap-out, but standing in front of me with her black wrap-around dress clinging to her thick frame, I could also tell that she knew how to keep it classy.

I would had never guessed that she was the same chick from the body shop. Never would had guessed that she was the same chick from that alley. She definitely had a nigga with a lot of questions, and I was going to make it a priority to get with her to ask them.

⚜

"So, how the fuck you gon' fix it?" I was standing in the middle of Lawrence's condo downtown, waiting for an answer that I knew he wouldn't be able to give me. "You just passed out a shit-load of drugs that's killing all the addicts that use that shit? How the fuck a nigga gon' sell that, Lawrence? In their eyes, you robbed them."

"I didn't rob shit. Fair exchange and fuckin' robbery."

He was standing at the room-length window admiring the view from his eighth-floor unit. His condo had a picture-perfect view of the bustling city below.

"Your right. Fair exchange ain't no robbery nigga, but that wasn't fair exchange. At least, I'm sure it doesn't feel like to them. *You* got paid and they didn't because they can't sell the shit you gave them. Just give them their fuckin' money back and you take the L."

Lawrence spun around from where he was standing and glared at me. It was like looking at the spitting image of myself except he was shorter, and his dreads were stiffer, thicker and styled different. While I wore mine neat and shoulder length, his resembled the styles in Florida. On some Kodak Black shit.

"Why the fuck would I do that?" he asked, glancing at me like I'd said something outlandish. Standing there in his silk pajamas, he swiveled around the short glass he was holding before putting it to his lips and taking a sip.

"Because you can afford the loss and they can't. The niggas we supplied done passed that shit out all over the place. Mid-level dealers. Street-level dealers. They can't afford to take the kind of losses that you can. Just do the right fuckin' thing," I grumbled, before walking off and taking a seat on the couch.

Dealing with Lawrence was becoming more and more difficult as each day passed. He and I were polar opposites. I stood on principles and his ass was lawless. He did what he wanted and didn't really care how anyone felt. I wasn't perfect but Lawrence was an entirely different man when it came to morale. It was as if he walked around angry all damn day. The only thing that made that nigga happy was the cocaine he liked to sniff but didn't think I knew about, and that bird bitch Casey that didn't want his ass. Only a nigga like Lawrence would go behind my back and cop some bullshit drugs, distribute it, and say fuck everybody after the fact. Even though he was my blood brother, it was difficult to like the nigga. I couldn't say that I did. I did however love him because we'd come out the same pussy.

"Fuck them niggas. I took a loss too. We all lost. I got more of that shit I can't get rid of just like they do. If anything, I should go murk the nigga that sold me that shit."

"It would help if you actually knew who the fuck it was, which I'm sure you don't because you were so busy being impatient and greedy, that you didn't do your homework. You not hurting for cash Lawrence. Just give them nigga's their money back." I was trying to get him to do the right thing by reasoning with him.

Lawrence scoffed. "So, you want me to pay niggas like Boobie, Tye, and Corey? Niggas that's eating good on the streets and can afford to take losses. Those niggas are the plugs on the streets. They not gonna go down line and pay everyone ther money back that they sold to. So, you tell me how the fuck that's democracy? Nah. Fuck that. I go to court in a couple days. Any one of them niggas that got a problem with what I gave them can see me 'bout it after that."

I couldn't understand how niggas could do shit and be dead ass wrong but be ready to go to war over it. I didn't bother responding so, Lawrence stared at me for a minute.

"Since you so concerned, you pay them," he suggested. "You the one with all the money. Do the right thing," he mocked me.

I stood to my feet. I was done talking to him, and frankly, I was about to be done with him entirely.

"I didn't get rich being greedy and unfair. I got rich because I made sure my team ate, and I was also good to them. You're right. I'll pay them. Only because they're technically my people, and anyone that knows me, knows that I do good fuckin' business. I'm not going to war over a petty wrong that you won't right, and I also don't want to be a target. When you're rich and those around you are starving, you become food."

"Yeah, whatever Dr. King," Lawrence grumbled, staring back out the window.

"Call me whatever you want, I'm leaving. But before I go, I do want to say this. Since they my people and you don't seem to give a fuck about them, you no longer have access to them. I'll let each and every one of those niggas that you sold those bull-shit drugs to know, that I could no longer vouch for any product you distribute. I also let niggas know that your independent as of the day you went behind my back and copped that bullshit."

Lawrence shot me a cold look but didn't say anything. He knew that by me informing Tye, Boobie and Corey of that, they weren't going to work with him. I only sold to those three people. If he didn't have any of them to work with, then he had no clients. I had single-handedly stopped his money source. Niggas didn't deal with Lawrence on the strength of his name. The dealt with him on the strength of mine. I had paved the way for his ass and as usual, the nigga refused to show an ounce of gratitude. I was the reason he was living the way he was living. And I didn't say that to brag. I was proud that I could build my family up. But the goal was to build them up so they could get out of the gutter. Unfortunately, Lawrence would get out of the gutter, but he couldn't shake the gutter mentality.

Lawrence had been the sole reason that I'd stayed in the game that long. I'd been wanting to get out of the game, only staying because he would find a way to talk me out of leaving. I wasn't in no mafia-style drug agreement. There was no 'only way out is death' for me. I could leave whenever I got ready.

"There's more to life than slinging fuckin' drugs and toting guns. You ain't poor no more bro," I reminded him. "We ain't in the trenches no more. You can't keep thinking like that. And I don't want to do this shit forever," I admitted. "Something tells me that the connect isn't moving any time soon, so I'm going to take advantage of that and tell him I'm throwing in my cards. I'm out bro. Literally and figuratively," I said before rising to my feet and heading out. "I suggest you do the same."

Lawrence didn't bother to respond. I knew that what I'd just done was going to put a big strain on our relationship. I couldn't stay on a boat that a nigga was poking holes in no way. If a nigga crossed niggas in the streets, then they had to watch their back. If a nigga crossed their own team, then they had more than their back to watch.

## ✣ 6 ✣

## ALIZE

The day had been long. I'd worked from nine in the morning and was just getting off at seven. I could now see why Lindsey had been so eager to hire my ass. She was overworked. I'd only been working there a few days but it seemed longer. I couldn't complain though. I was thankful actually. After Neal bonded me out, I started job searching the very next day. Luxe Car Collection was one of the first places I sent my sorry excuse for a resume to. A few hours later, Lindsey was calling me for an interview. I showed up the next day and after answering a few questions, she'd literally hired me on the spot. I now knew why. Lindsey had just graduated high school and was ready to travel and enjoy herself. The only way that she would be able to do that was if she had someone trained and able to fill her shoes.

I didn't have a problem with running things as long as I was trained to do so. My issue was that Luxe was open six days a week, ten hours a day. Lance or Lindsey needed to hire another person if she was going to be leaving soon, because I wasn't working no damn sixty-hours a week. I wanted money but I didn't want to work all day and night for it either.

I gathered up my things from my desk and got prepared to

leave. I figured, before I headed to the bus stop that I would talk to Lance really quick about what was expected of me. I needed a set schedule that didn't consist of sixty-hour weeks. It was bad enough that I was barely seeing my girls. Judy lived way out in Decatur, while my motel was way in Forest Park. It was only thirty-minutes by vehicle, but it was more than an hour each way by bus.

I headed to the back and tapped lightly on Lance's office door. After hearing him tell me to come in, I pushed the door all the way open.

"Hey, Lance. You got a minute?" I asked, peeking in.

"For you?" he flashed a warm smile. "Hell yeah. Sit down."

I walked in and took a seat in one of the two empty office chairs directly across from him. I didn't know why, but Lance made me nervous. He didn't act like a boss per say. He just acted like a regular hood guy that I just happened to work for. He wasn't what one would consider professional. He was laid back most of the time and joked around a great deal of the day. It was only when he got into that office that he seemed to harden and become more serious. I had a feeling he was complex man. That he was fighting demons that folks didn't know shit about. Lindsey had told me, when I saw him in his office, to try not to bother him. He handled unsaid business back there and also served as his little sanctuary. I could understand that since he had it nice and cozy. He had expensive-looking paintings lining the wall, a large leather sofa tucked in the corner, and a huge desk that probably cost an easy couple grand. A few beautiful silk plants and gold-themed office décor completed the look.

Lance didn't think I remembered him, but I did. He used to run the streets of Lakewood Heights back when I was a pre-teen running around with a cracked-out mama. Of course, he looked different. He didn't have a head full of dreads and he didn't have that same thick physique, but I knew it was him once I heard the name and got a good look at his face. I wasn't even gon' lie, Lance was fine as hell. To the point where I just wanted to touch all over him. Touch his body and see if he felt as good as he looked. So fine, it made me nervous. It was borderline excitement and I was literally crushing on him. Anytime my eyes fell on him, my heart started racing and I got to breathing all hard. My panties would start to moisten. It was crazy since I'd only been with one man other than Neal. No man had ever excited me. Not until Lance.

"Whatchu wanna holla at me about?" he asked, gazing at me. He seemed to enjoy giving me his undivided attention.

"Well, I know I've only been here a few days. I'm getting the swing of things. I pretty much have the procedures down. But Lindsey's been training me very fast and I'm assuming it's because she's leaving soon?" I asked, already knowing the answer to the question.

"Right. My mother's letting her travel a little bit since she graduated at the top of her class and is heading to college in the fall."

"And she's leaving for more than a month, right?"

"Yep. Maybe longer. She's helped me out a great deal for a long time. I don't want to make her feel like she's obligated to continue doing so. I want her to enjoy herself. She's earned it."

"I definitely agree with that, but Lance, how are you gonna run this place six days a week with one clerk?" I asked.

"You don't think I can run my own place?" he asked before laughing. "Damn. I expected you to have more faith in me Alize."

"Oh, my bad. I didn't know. I didn't expect you to actually come out front and help out, especially since you stay cooped up in this office all day."

Lance studied me with a flirty grin that made me instantly uncomfortable. "Oh, you be checking for a nigga?"

"N-No. Not at all. I just thought maybe you be busy back here."

"Sometimes I am busy. Giving attention to shit that's undeserving. But you'll see in the next few days that'll I'll be redirecting my attention elsewhere."

His eyes traveled up and down my body shamelessly. He definitely was flirting and showing blatant appreciation for a bitch's presence, but it was the way that he said shit when he said it. It was so fucking smooth and seductive. Even the most basic shit had me ready to drop down like I was Meg The Stallion. I had to get the fuck out of that nigga office before I hopped on his dick.

"Cool." That was all I could think to say. Out of all the things to say, I said that dumb shit.

"Anything else you needed to ask? Anything you need? Let me know how I can be of assistance." He was doing the shit again. Saying shit to get a rise out of me. I wore my emotions on my sleeve, and I knew damn well that nigga could see the effect he had on me. The attraction was crazy.

"Actually, Lance, I do have one more question. Is the reason why you're so comfortable talking low-key slick and talking to me like you know me because you knew my mama?" I asked.

Like I said before, it took me a little minute to recognize Lance at first. After all, I was only eleven the last time I saw him. He had to of been at least fifteen or sixteen. Old enough to remember my face and name. I was a little thicker, but I still looked the same. I knew he remembered me, and I wanted him to acknowledge it. I wasn't ashamed of my past. I went through what I went through, and I didn't want him thinking that he couldn't talk about certain shit around me or bring certain things up.

"Actually, it is," he said with zero hesitation. "I definitely knew ya mom and I remember you," he admitted.

"I thought so. I just asked that because if I'm going to be working here then I don't want none of that awkward energy between us. I'm not ashamed of nothing," I said before getting up and sliding my chair in so that I could leave.

"But I gotta go, I gotta catch my bus."

"You don't have a car?" he asked. Lance stood up and grabbed his keys off the table.

"It was stolen a couple of weeks ago, but I'm good. I usually catch an Uber or ride the bus."

"You didn't file a claim? And I'll take you home. Come on," he said. He walked around me and pulled the door open for me to walk through.

"Yeah, I had insurance, but I only had liability."

"Ohhhh."

"So, that's how you got to the interview?" he asked.

"Yeah, I caught an Uber. It's just that where I'm staying, those Uber's start to add up. So, sometimes I switch it up and just catch the bus."

"Well, you definitely won't be catching any buses while working for me. It isn't safe. I'll make sure you have a way home from now on since you'll be here to seven and I'll be leaving out anyway. And in the future, we might be able to get you a work vehicle."

"You don't have to do any of that. And as far as that ride, I live way out in Forest Park."

"I know I don't have to do anything. I want to do it. Besides, it'll give us a little time to talk. Catch up about people we used to know."

Lance set the alarm, locked everything up, and then led the way to where he was parked in the parking lot.

"This me," he said, walking up to a big, black Denali. Before I could touch the handle of the door, he stopped me.

"You don't open car doors when you ridin' with a real nigga." He flashed a goofy grin and I climbed in. I could get used to Lance's big, black fine ass.

⚜

With no traffic, the ride home was brief. Lance and I still managed to catch up on everything and everybody from the hood. We knew a lot of the same people, and surprisingly, shared a lot of things in common.

"I can't believe Peanut is your mom." I threw my hand up to my mouth and giggled. The only reason I laughed was because Peanut was crazy. Her and my mother had scrapped a few times back in the day. I now realized why Lance had argued with Black in the alleyway about his treatment of my mother. His mother was also a crackhead running wild. Since Lawrence was older, it didn't seem to affect him as much.

"Yeah, she was crazy as hell back in the day. Still is. She just turned her life around after some tragic shit happened. Went to rehab and changed her life. When I came into a little money, I moved all of us out to the sticks and she been good. She a real-life church lady now," he said before staring out the window.

"That's great. I'm proud of her. I wish my mom would have gotten it together." I sighed. "I guess everything happens for a reason though right."

"Absolutely," he said, tearing his gaze away from the highway and giving me a forced smile.

"You okay?" I asked.

"Yeah. Why you ask that?" His brows rose in curiosity.

"I don't know." I shrugged. "You just zoned out when you spoke of your mama."

"Just thought about a couple things, is all. I'm good."

Right after he said that his GPS was letting him know that he'd arrived at the shabby motel that I called home.

"So, if you don't mind me asking, why you staying at a motel? What happened to your place?"

I paused for a moment and thought about telling him it was none of his business. But for some reason, I felt comfortable talking to Lance. I had a feeling that he genuinely just wanted to know.

"It's a long story, but I walked in on my kids father fucking the neighbor in our bed. You remember the goofy ass nigga that I was arguing with back at Boobie's?"

Lance nodded.

"Well, after I caught them, I lost it and fired on they asses."

"What!" he asked all loud in disbelief. "You banged on em?" he asked, his eyes widening.

I dropped my head in embarrassment.

"I did. And even though I was angry, I regret it. I got evicted behind that mess. Dropped that nigga immediately. He wasn't worth it, and I ain't to taking losses behind anybody. Especially not no dog ass nigga. But on some real shit, I take commitment seriously. If I fuck with you that's what it is. You get loyalty. He showed me that he doesn't honor that type of shit, so I said fuck him. Shit went downhill for me after that, but things'll get better." I shrugged.

"So, you're single?" Lance asked, like he was happy to hear it.

"Yeah, I'm single." I looked forward and fought back the urge to smile.

"Well, I'm glad to hear that," Lance said seductively. "So glad to hear that," he added.

"Boy, shut up." I laughed for the hundredth time since I'd been in that truck.

I couldn't help but think about the fact that it had been a while since I last laughed. I didn't know if I was ready to get out and start dating, but I certainly wouldn't mind getting to know a little bit more about Lance. He seemed to be thinking the same thoughts.

"Well, I'm gonna head in. Gotta get up early and get back to work in the morning. Thanks again for the ride."

"You think I can see you again outside of work?" he asked, before I could touch the handle of the door. While he stared at me and waited for a response, I couldn't help but admire his features. He was just black and perfect. He even smelled good. The scent of Tom Ford was wafting off his body and tickling my nose every time he moved his thick, taut body.

"I'm not sure if that's a good idea," I said, surprising my damn self since I didn't want to say that. The thing was, I needed to get into a place, and since Neal was still in line to help me, I didn't want anything fucking that up.

Lindsey was a sweet girl, but she was the typical meddling sister that also happened to have a motor-mouth. She'd already filled me in on Lance's situation with his ex. She'd already advised me that Lance didn't date like typical hood-guys. Never had. He wanted a connection. Needed one. If he was interested in someone, he was focused, determined, and persistent. *He likes you. I can tell,'* is what she told me. And she was spot on. I just hoped that he could be patient with me. I had to make sure my girls were straight first.

"And why don't you think it's a good idea?" he asked as if he were repeating himself. Lost in a brief thought, I probably didn't hear him.

"Because ... even though Neal and I aren't together, I need to get along with him right now. For reasons I don't want to talk about," I said so he wouldn't start asking a bunch of questions. "You and Boobie do business together and Neal is his cousin. You all have interacted. If you and I were to hang out or be seen together, it might cause some tension. Tension that I literally can't afford right now."

He nodded. "I respect that."

"Well, goodnight. And thanks again." I reached for the door handle again, but he stopped me.

"What I tell you earlier?" He opened his door, hopped out, and then came around to let me out.

"While you sort out those issues, you got, I'll be around. I'll see you tomorrow Alize," he said before heading back around to the driver's side.

I walked off and let out a deep breath that I felt like I'd been holding in. *Lawd have mercy*, I thought to myself. I was definitely going to get things in order. I not only wanted my girls back, but Lord knows, I wanted Lance's ass bad.

## 7

## LANCE

After dropping Alize off after work night after night, my dick was always hard as a missile. It didn't take long. Like I said before, I believed in fate. She was it. Gorgeous, smart and humble. But most of all, she could relate to my past. A past that we damn near shared. I didn't know who the fuck Neal was, but I knew he had fucked up. Because once I got ahold of Alize, she was mine. She was perfect. Not only that but her little ass was crazy. She knew how to use a gun and would actually pull that shit. It was just crazy to see because she was always so sweet and professional when working. It was nice to know that she was a woman who could turn the fuck up when people got out of line. I wasn't sure why that turned me on, but it did. I loved classy women that could check you without violence as well, but it was just something about a female that was a little wild.

There was just something different about shawty. Something that I didn't often see in a chick from the projects or a chick from the hood. She wanted more for herself and she didn't mind working for it. Every day she caught an Uber to work and every day she was on time. She always had a positive attitude despite living in a motel and dealing with unspoken trauma from the life she'd lived with her mother. She never spoke on it, but I knew it was there just like it was for me.

Alize could've had a nigga financing her; yet she was more focused on getting her own. She was going to be my wife. I didn't care that she had kids. She didn't seem like the type to have no disrespectful children no way. I also didn't care about that nigga Neal or Boobie's ass. She'd spoken about not wanting any tension, but that's how I knew that she had never dealt with a real nigga before. If Neal were to be a problem, he would be *my* problem. Men handled men. And I wouldn't have a problem checking either of them. While she might not have known how I did things, niggas through Atlanta did. I would light some shit up. Over and over, until my point was made.

I stopped accepting disrespect long ago, and if for some reason a nigga tried me, I wouldn't hesitate to check his ass. Especially for a loved one. And for some reason, I had a feeling that I was going to love Alize.

⚜

"What do you think about Lindsey switching schools?" I asked my mama.

I was laid back on her big, red sectional, feet perched up, eating a plate of fried catfish and grits. I didn't get to see mama much because I was always on the move during the week, but every Sunday, I made it my business to get to her big ass house in Marietta so I could eat good and curl up on her furniture.

"Don't drop that shit on my couch," she said sharply before sitting down beside me. It didn't matter that I bought it, so I didn't even bother saying it.

"Dang, Ma. You gon' sink the couch in." I laughed after feeling that motherfucker shift when she plopped her wide ass down.

'Fuck you, Lance. I ain't that damn big. And why you ask me about Lindsey switching schools?" Her face grew serious. She knew that I moved strategically and when I said some shit, it had merit to it.

"Lawrence is moving grimy. Nobody can tell him nothing, and I don't want her in Atlanta." That was all the details that I was going to give her.

"Moving grimy, huh? You think she'd be a target?"

"I do. She's all over the business Instagram. A lot of niggas know her as our sister. Especially because she stay tagging us in stupid shit. My brothers this, my brothers that. I don't want niggas knowing who's who in our life."

"Well, it's too late for all that. You know Lindsey is a social media baby. That's the thing for their generation. But I'll let her know," she said before reaching down on the coffee table, grabbed the remote and cut on the tv.

"You telling her or asking her?" I eyed her while she flicked through a few channels. My mother had changed so much. She used to be so skinny that she looked sick. When she walked around, her hair used to be going in every direction. Sometimes she would skip baths for days because all she was worried about was getting high. I remembered that Lawrence and I used to fight each and every time someone tried to disrespect her. Unlike a lot of folks, we didn't see her as a crackhead first. We saw her as our mama. She just had a drug addiction. She was one of those crackheads that would let a motherfucker know that she was about to go get her boys. And when we came back there was never any talking.

I had always stepped for those that I love, regardless of their condition. She turned her life around when she knew that it was time for her to do the same thing. The sober Peanut had been drugfree for over a decade. She was now healthy, glowing and liked to wear eight-hundred-dollar wigs by Alonzo Arnold. My mama was my heart.

"I'm gon' motherfuckin' tell her Lance!" she yelled, causing me to burst out laughing. My mama was loud and ghetto. I was definitely being sarcastic the day that I told Alize my mama was a church lady. It didn't matter how rich I got. She would literally curse, yell and run through her big ass house.

"Ma, why are you yelling?"

"Because you acting like I don't run shit. If it isn't safe for her black ass to be in Atlanta, then she won't be in Atlanta. She got into both Spelman and Howard. She can go to Howard."

"Way in DC?" I frowned.

"It's either that or Atlanta, Lance."

She got up off the couch abruptly. "Shit, I might go with her for a while. I ain't trying to get caught up behind Lawrence shit either. And neither should you," she scolded. "You been carrying this motherfuckin' family for as long as I can remember. I had to change and so does he. Son or no son. He not taking everybody down behind his short, black ass."

I couldn't help but chuckle. She talked shit but it was always real. And she was right. Everybody changed except him. There was nothing for Lindsey to change since I'd been up since she was little. Her life had been smooth sailing for the most part. She didn't remember our mother being on drugs or living in the hood.

"I'm going to lay down. My damn stomach hurts."

"You be eating too much, Ma." I laughed before leaning up and sliding my plate onto the table.

"Nigga you eat too much. Don't worry 'bout what I eat," she laughed. "I'm going to sleep, so I love you and make sure you put that plate in the sink, so I don't have to slap the shit out you."

"You gotta catch me first," I joked.

⚬⚙⚬

"Let me take you to dinner," I said to Alize as I leaned against her desk after I had locked the front door, right at closing.

Even though it was a Monday night, I was bored, and I really wanted to kick it with her. I enjoyed her company and frankly, I really wanted to keep spending time with her, keep getting her comfortable enough to the point that she would fuck with a nigga.

"Lance, I already told you that I don't think that's a good idea."

She grabbed her little Coach bag from off the desk and began preparing to leave. As good as she was looking, there was no way that I was about to give up that easy. That day she had on an emerald-green jersey dress with a plunging neckline that showed off her sun-kissed, brown skin. That little bob she wore was cascading down her face and resting on her collarbone.

Despite her telling me that she didn't want to go, I knew that she really did. She had warmed up to me a lot. We spent a lot of time together. Even though we did mostly work shit, we would still laugh and cut up with the occasional flirting. I was growing tired of that. It wasn't enough. I wanted her on a deeper level. I wanted to be the one that helped her enjoy herself and minimize the stress in her life. Treat her to shit like dinner, a movie, or a spa date. Shit, I would take her on a helicopter ride or fucking cabin in the mountains. I just wanted her to relax and not worry about shit. Experience things that I knew none of the niggas she was with before did.

"Please," I asked. I wasn't trying to be on no begging shit. A nigga just wasn't used to taking no for an answer.

Alize sighed. "Only if I can choose the place."

"Sounds good to me," I said.

◑✦◐

I wasn't surprised that Alize picked a soul food restaurant nearby called Nana's. It was a spot that she admitted to frequenting often. It was a quaint, little spot with shit like collard greens, cornbread, and sweet tea. It was cheap but it was good as hell. Just her selecting that restaurant made me dig her even more. It was small things like that I noticed in women. She wasn't trying to dig all in a nigga pockets even though she probably knew I had the money. She just wanted to eat good. And that's exactly what her greedy ass did.

"Yo, you greedy like my mama." I laughed while stuffing some cornbread in my mouth and washing it down with some iced tea.

"Boy, please. I barely ate today. It was busy up in there but yo' ass wouldn't know because you were back in your office on the couch sleep."

I damn near spit my drink out. "Don't be watching me shawty." I laughed.

"You look too good not to watch," she said, catching me all the way off guard. "Yooo, chill," I said. I was too black to blush, but she had a nigga face hot.

"You pop slick to me all day, but you can't take a lil' compliment? Let me find out." She stabbed at her plate, loaded a bunch of shit together on her fork, and then stuffed it in her mouth.

"Well, I know who better be able to cook, because you damn sure can eat." She shrugged and paid me no mind. At least she chewed with her mouth closed.

"I sure can," she finally replied after swallowing her food.

"How you manage to keep your figure?"

"Hereditary. My mama had a nice little body before the drugs."

"Yeah, I remember."

As soon as I said it, I regretted it. Alize grew quiet, and an awkward silence followed that. That shit sounded fucked up. Especially because of how the perverted ass niggas in the hood used to do her.

"That came out fucked up. I didn't mean it like that. I'm sorry."

"You good."

I knew I had struck a nerve because she was still quiet. I was hoping that she wasn't looking at a nigga like a pervert or nothing.

"I know you wasn't one of those types Lance," Alize said, finally breaking the silence between us. "I remember how you tried to speak up for her that day in the alley. That was some crazy shit you know. That nigga Black was disgusting. Whatever happened to that nigga anyway? When I got took from my mama at eleven, I went to stay with my aunt and I never saw that nigga again."

Hearing Black's name caused me to tense up. There was a saying that killers were either born or made. I had been made. It was weird because Black was my very first murder. That one was the one that sat on my conscience. Everyone after that meant less and less.

"I heard he got killed."

"Aww damn." Alize paused for a minute. "I'm sure he deserved it."

"So, you think that killing is okay? You think there are times when a person's life is okay to be taken."

Alize paused and sighed. I knew she was thinking critically. Carefully selecting her choice of words.

"I don't think killing is right; however, sometimes it's necessary. Sometimes you don't have a choice. There are so many different factors. Would I kill someone for violating my children? Yes, I would. Would I just take a life for nothing? No, I wouldn't. But using Black as an example. Black was one of those people that did shit that was spiteful and hateful. Things that could push people over the edge. Even though he wasn't a powerful man, he was in a position of power in the hood. He had power over a lot of the younger guys and power over the addicts. He abused that power daily. You saw that. I guess somebody got tired of that shit. Like I said, killing is wrong ... but sometimes it's necessary."

"I can live with that answer." Hearing her response had me sitting there staring at her, looking dumb as a bitch. She was what I wanted and needed.

"Look shawty, I'm gonna keep it real with you. There's something about you ... Actually, there's a lot about you. I need someone like you in my life."

Alize's face grew serious, and her eyes gazed into mine as I spoke. I guess she wanted to see and hear the authenticity.

"Every female that I've ran into didn't want shit but my money. They couldn't relate to me and they didn't care to. They didn't understand struggle. Didn't value grind. You have all those qualities. You know a nigga want you, but you haven't asked me for shit. All you ask is for me to let you get your shit together. You never switched your energy. Never focused on what I could do for you, even when you knew a nigga was willing. You instead worked for me, earning your money from the contribution you make. That says a lot about you. I fuck witchu shawty. I want you to fuck wit me. On some intimate shit. The physical attraction is insane, and I connect with you on a mental level. I just want ya time. I want a chance."

I laid that shit right the fuck out on the table. I didn't have time for games, and I didn't want to give her the chance to run back to her fuck ass baby daddy. All she needed was me. I was gon' change her life.

"I've never had no one think that highly of me. On some real shit, I'm flattered."

"So, is that a yes?" I asked.

"Why this sound like elementary school?" She laughed, showing both rows of teeth. "Do you like me. Yes or no."

I couldn't help but chuckle at her childish ass. Despite her attempt to change the subject with humor, I wasn't having it.

"What's holding you back, Alize? What's keeping you from me?"

She paused and her expression changed from happy to bleak. She reached down and grabbed a napkin off the table.

"I'm sorry. I don't want to cry, but I can't help it."

"Talk to me. I might be able to help."

She grew quiet and dabbed at her damp eyes. Her lip was quivering so she drew in a deep breath. "Lance, I just got a lot going on. I lost my kids, okay. After I got kicked out, I stayed with my Aunt Melva for a while. Some shit happened and she told me I had to go. I moved into the room where I'm at now. I got a little job at Walmart and since I didn't' have a sitter, I left them alone in the room by themselves. They got scared one night during a thunderstorm and called 911. They sent officers by there and just like that, they were gone."

While that wasn't a smart move, I understood her plight. Growing up in the hood, a lot of folks left their kids at home while they worked.

"I'm sorry to hear that, Alize."

"You must think I'm a bad mom." She sniffled, her head dropping some and eyes lowering to the table.

"Yo, lift your head up. You have nothing to be ashamed of. Especially when you talking to me." I watched as she brought her head up so her eyes could level with mine. "And no, I don't think you're a bad mother. You made a bad choice, but you're not a bad mom. I know a lot of people that's happened to and they don't hold a torch to you as a person."

Alize's face softened and a reluctant smile appeared.

"What can I help you with, Alize? I know you don't want help, but I'm not taking no for an answer. I have it, and I want to do it."

She didn't respond right away.

"I don't have any ulterior motives. All I'm trying to do is put you in a better space. Make your life better. A car? A deposit for an apartment? What can I help you with?"

"Well, Neal was going to help me with a place."

"Yeah, but at what cost?" I eyed her curiously.

"He wants to get back together. I told him I'd consider it after he helped me move into a place." I admired and appreciated her honesty.

Even though she was coming with some baggage, she was willingly admitting to the fact that she wasn't perfect.

"Do you want to be with him?" I asked.

"Hell naw. I just said that so I could get my girls in a place."

"Okay." I nodded and studied her briefly. "So, let him know

that you don't want him and don't need his help. I'll take care of all of that. I'll get you into a place so you can get your girls back. I'll let you use one of the cars at Luxe until we get you into one later, and I'll also get you a lawyer for family court."

"I can't ask you to do all of that," Alize said.

"Why?"

"Because it's too much. I know you have a business and you got money, but I don't want to come into your life just taking. I want to be able to give to," she said, briefly looking back down again.

"You are giving. You're giving me happiness. Peace. Something that a nigga ain't had in a while. And I'm not hurting for cash Alize. Whatever you need, you got it. Ya problems are big but they can be fixed. Now ... is that a yes or no? You gon' fuck with a nigga or not?"

Her lips curled up like she was in thought. And then she started laughing. "Hell yeah, I'ma fuck witchu," she said, mocking me.

❧

Once we finished eating, we talked and laughed while we walked out the restaurant and headed to the parking lot that we'd parked in. The sound of footsteps behind us caused me to reach for my gun.

"Oh, so this what we doing?" a disgruntled voice called out closely behind us as we were walking down the sidewalk and heading back to the parking lot.

I grabbed Alize's hand so that we could pause a moment and face the man of the recognizable voice. We spun around and I actually spotted not one, but two familiar faces in front of me. Still holding her hand, I gave it a light squeeze to let her know that I would handle things.

"Wassup, Boobie?" I greeted my long-time acquaintance.

Even though I was friendly, I eyed him curiously since the

two of them had walked up like there was some type of unspoken hostility. The tension was thick in the air. I turned my gaze to the other nigga he was with. Yeah, I recognized the nigga but frankly, I didn't give a fuck. He wasn't my nigga. I had no relationship with him whatsoever, so I wasn't sure what the fuck could be the problem. But then I remembered that Alize had been stringing his fuck ass along so that she could get into a crib. I looked to my side and she was literally standing there like a deer in headlights. I couldn't say that she looked scared. She just looked like she was more at a loss for words.

"Wassup." I began snapping my fingers like folks did when they couldn't remember something and was trying hard as hell.

"Neal," he stated evenly. The nigga glared at me with a 'cut the bullshit' face.

"Right, Neal. Wassup," I replied, unimpressed with his smug attitude.

Neal didn't reply right away. He instead eyed Alize with intense animosity before smirking. He then turned his attention back to me and responded.

"Nothing much. Just trying to figure out why you out here with my daughter's mother. Did you know she was my shawty?" he asked, turning his gaze to me.

Alize went to speak but I held my hand up and stopped her.

"Nigga I don't even know you, so I'm not gonna sit here and tell you that I really gave a fuck. It wasn't an issue for me. It was an issue for her, but I assured that if it became a problem, then we would discuss it like men. Any chick with me don't do too much worrying."

I noticed Neal's' jaws tighten. I was hoping he spoke whatever feelings he had that were all bottled up. I always had time. And if I didn't have time, I could make time.

"Lance let me holla at you for a minute?"

"Yeah, go talk to him, so I can rap to my baby mama," Neal said sharply.

I stared at him for a minute.

"Nigga, I don't take orders from workers," I replied coolly.

Embarrassment flooded Neal's face and anger quickly followed behind it. I looked him over. He wasn't big at all and I had no doubt that I would beat the shit out of him. Then again, he would probably pull his gun first. Considering that we were in a pretty area of downtown Atlanta, I figured punching him in his face was too risky. Most men were prideful. He would have definitely started blazing if I smacked him up in front of his boss and baby's mama. I looked at Alize, and I could tell that she wasn't feeling the whole little friendly standoff. She looked very uneasy.

"Boobie, you know I don't have no issue with you. You can get with me on a later date."

I looked back at Alize and then addressed Neal.

"I don't think she wants to talk, so she doesn't have to. So, both you niggas have a good night."

I slipped my hand into hers and began walking with her by my side, leaving the both of them standing behind me quiet. Boobie knew me personally. He knew how I got down. I was a cool nigga. I could be a great ally, but I could be a vicious ass enemy. I wasn't worried about them coming behind us. I had already declared the conversation dead so that's what it was.

When we got to my Denali in the parking lot, I opened the door for her to climb in. Boobie and Neal were walking off and back the way they came from. I stood there for a second and noticed Neal glance back a few times. I knew he didn't like Alize's new situation, but if he knew better, he would respect it.

## 8

### ALIZE

Lance and I had only been dating a few weeks, but in those few weeks, he had walked in and made my life so much easier. Responding to that Craigslist job ad had been the best decision I had made. It had literally changed my life. Well, not completely but damn near. Gone were the fights, shootings, and trash strewn parking lots. There were no more bitches hanging out in droopy bonnets, worrying about the next chick. No more drug-addicts walking up on me trying to sell me something. All that shit was gone. I had a new apartment, and I was about to start a new life.

Earlier that day, Lance had personally taken me to pick up the keys to my new apartment in Buckhead. The shit was lit. A tennis-court, fitness center, and even a pool and playground for my kids. It was nothing for him to swipe his card and pay my rent up for an entire year. A whole fucking year. And the nigga hadn't walked in with a bookbag full of cash. He had walked in there like the man that he was and swiped his bank card. If I hadn't seen it with my own eyes, I wouldn't have believed the it. The icing on the cake was the final conversation I had with Lindsey before she left. She knew all the things her brother was doing for me and she seemed genuinely happy for me. I told her it seemed like too much too soon, but she brushed me off. "Girl, that's just him. If he fucks with you, he fucks with you. And besides, that nigga is a real life millionaire. It's small to him. Let him do what he does best. Look out for the people he fucks with."

Hearing that Lance was a millionaire was almost surreal. I damn near couldn't believe it. Eventually, my braid accepted it. Most bitches would had said, I'd hit the jackpot, but I didn't see it that way. I was a firm believer in God and fate. I was blessed. Lance was a good man. We got along beautifully, he wasn't negative, he didn't put me down, and he did everything in his power to make sure that I was always good. I didn't have to ask. If he saw there was a need, then he was taking care of shit. 'That's what men do', he'd always tell me. That shit made me want to fucking scream. Despite how good to me he was, we hadn't even gotten around to sex yet. He didn't seem pressed for it. He was more focused on making sure I was good and that I had my girls back.

Speaking of my girls, Neal had even seemed to be changing his tune. I wasn't sure if Lance had actually met up with Boobie or not, but since the night we'd stumbled into them after leaving Nana's, I had still been able to continue seeing my girls and spending time with them. Of course, Neal would inquire about the extent of my relationship with Lance but I would never go into details. I didn't want anyone speaking on shit that I was doing. wanted them with me badly, but I knew they were in good hands with Judy. During the day they would attend a little daycare that Neal had set up for them. I, of course, went in and observed it, making sure things looked good. Things were really looking up. Lance had made good on the promise of a lawyer and I had a hearing in a few days. According to the lawyer, I would likely be getting the girls back that day. I was so happy I was near tears.

Although I had just gotten the keys to my new place, I had bedroom furniture scheduled for delivery later that day. Lance was going to fill in for me at the business while I waited for the deliverymen to arrive. What he didn't know was that I was also planning something special for him and I. I knew he didn't want to force me into sex, but I really cared about Lance. He was good to me in so many ways, and I wanted us to be intimate. To be frank, a bitch wanted to see what his sexy black ass was working with.

I'd stayed at his condo multiple nights and even slept beside him in the same bed; however, he never made a move. He'd always just kiss on me and hold me. I was tired of that. I wanted to be fucked.

"Babe, I'm leaving," I called out from my desk. Even though he took me to pick up the keys, he'd brought me back to the car I was driving. Since he owned a fleet of vehicles, he let me drive one of the ones that he had just taken from the available line up. It wasn't anything wrong with it, he just liked to rotate his vehicles after they got a certain amount of miles on them. Imagine going from a Hyundai to a two-year-old Jaguar F-Type. I was riding so clean I could shit on hoes if I went through the hood. Especially Melissa or Melvina's stinking asses. The crazy part was, even though I could have, I didn't. Lance had handed me the keys and said to keep it until we get me into something new. The morale of the story was, I didn't care about stuntin' on anyone. I didn't care about proving a point. All I cared about was getting my kids back and building with Lance.

After calling out to Lance for the second time, he finally emerged around the corner from his office.

"I heard you, babe. I told you I was coming," he said, before leaning in and pressing his thick, soft lips into mine. I wanted to tongue him down in the middle of the floor, but I resisted. I would do all that later.

"What's all this for?" Lance beamed as he stepped into the bedroom of my new apartment.

"I just wanted to do a little something nice for you," I told him, before spinning around so he could admire the two-piece lingerie set that I'd ordered online from Victoria's Secret, just for him.

"A little?" he said sarcastically. He threw his hands around me and cupped my ass cheeks while he pulled me into him. "Ain't nothing little about this," he joked, before leaning down and kissing me.

I wasted no time slipping my tongue into his mouth. I'd already had my shot of liquid courage before he'd came. I wanted to be bold and ready to initiate things if I had to. Luckily for me, Lance already seemed to be on the same page. His thick rod was rock hard and pressing into my stomach

"Damn, girl," he said, pulling away from me. "I see you ready ain't you."

"Yes, daddy," I panted. The liquor was talking.

"You sure?" Lance asked. He lifted me up and threw my legs around his body so he could carry me to my brand new bed that we were about to bless.

"I'm sure," I replied.

Lance had me swimming in my own juices. My clit was throbbing, and I wanted him badly. I didn't want to seem like a hoe, but I'd been waiting for that moment. Waiting for the minute he showed me every precious inch of the dick he was gonna fill me up with.

Lance got me to the edge of the bed and placed me down gently. He began to slowly undress. He pulled his shirt off and exposed his thick, tight chest. I couldn't help myself. I rose up and began licking all over him, gently kissing him too.

"Damn you exited." He laughed. "You got a nigga brick in this bitch. Mouth all wet. What else that thang do?" he asked, before pulling off his pants. He stood there in his Ethika boxer briefs, dick curved and bulging from them. Like the bad girl I was, I reached out and rubbed it gently.

"You pull them off and I'll show you," I replied.

Lance slipped off those boxers and I said a silent prayer to God. I'd prayed for a good man on many nights, but He had outdone himself. Lance was perfect. His dick was long, thick and veiny like a Snicker bar. My mouth fell right onto it. I licked, slurped and spelled my name all over that dick. Lance ran his fingers through my hair and massaged my scalp while I inhaled and exhaled his dick like a porn star.

"Shit, Alize, baby," he cooed. "You gon' make a nigga cum all over the place," he admitted in a breathy voice.

Just as he started to stiffen up, he pulled himself away and pushed me back on the bed. He pulled my legs over his shoulder, gripped my thighs, and then buried his head in my pussy.

My mouth fell open and I proceeded to squirm, wiggle and cry out until I was creaming all up in his mouth. While I basked in euphoric ecstasy, I held his dreads up in the air like I was about to put his hair in a ponytail. Lance licked me dry, blew on it to cool it off, and then licked me wet all over again so he could enter me with ease.

When Lance pushed his dick inside of me, I felt myself come again. He was thick and long, but he eventually tunneled his way through, and my pussy expanded to accommodate his girth.

I came several times that night as Lance fucked me missionary, doggy-style and while holding me up in the air. I swear he was everything that I'd ever fucking wanted. By the time we were finished and wrapped in each other's sweaty arms, I was feeling some type of way. A way I hadn't felt in a long ass time. Lance was special, and I knew that it wouldn't be long before I was telling the nigga 'come in me, daddy,' or 'I love you.'

## ✿ 9 ✿

## ALEXIS

W hen I strolled into Luxe Car Collection, I wasn't expecting to see a new bitch sitting behind the front desk. Luckily, I had my shades covering my eyes so she couldn't spot the look of shock and disapproval in my face.

"Hi, welcome to Luxe," the little, receptionist bitch said all happily.

She stood up to greet me, and I couldn't help but study her and give her a thorough once over. She was cute. A natural thick broad with pretty pecan skin. Next to me, she was kind of average, but had the potential to be super bad if she wanted to. That fact actually scared me. She reminded me of everything that Lance wanted me to be, but I wasn't. I decided that I wasn't going to get too far ahead of myself. If I could just get Lance alone and talk with him for a little bit, I had no doubt that I would be able to wheel his ass back in.

"Are you looking to rent a vehicle?" the receptionist asked me, tearing me away from my thoughts of Lance's fine, rich ass, who I desperately wanted the fuck back.

"What brings you in?"

She was starting to get on my damn nerves. She was acting

like a pushy ass saleslady. I looked at her and rolled my eyes. *What brings you in.* I mocked her fake, professional sounding voice in my head.

I removed my Chanel shades so she could see my face when I spoke. "What's your name, sweetheart?" I asked her.

"My name is Alize."

"Alize, huh? Cute," I said smugly. "Well, Alize, I'm a friend of the owner. If you don't mind me asking ... Who hired you?"

"Why does that matter?" she asked, her tone switching from sweet and professional to stern and ghetto. It actually kind of surprised me. I couldn't help but smirk. *Lance must have hired this hoodrat.* It was right up his alley. He was from the hood and was always trying to surround himself with a bunch of peasants and motherfuckers who didn't mind slaving away all day. He had to be fucking her.

"I'm sorry, sweetie. I was just asking."

"Well, *Alexis*, if you must know, Lindsey hired me, not Lance. But you could have just asked me that," she said sharply.

"How do you know my name?"

"That shows that you don't pay attention to things that actually matter, like names. I'm Melvina's cousin. But, as you can see, I also work here now. Lance isn't here though, and even though you wouldn't tell me what you need, I'm assuming that you aren't interested in renting a vehicle. You're just interested in Lance. Would you like for me to take a message and see if he's willing to get back to you?" she said, her tone a tad bit nastier that time.

*Yeah, he's definitely fucking this bitch.*

I suddenly remembered the smart mouth bitch. *Alize.* Yeah, I'd met her once or twice at one of Melvina's family functions. She'd always had a quiet, fiery spirit. What concerned me was that she had way too much sizzle that day. Lance was generous and his fuck game was exceptional. So, if he was fucking a simple little broad like Alize, I knew that she wasn't going to willingly let him go.

I decided to change my approach. I was about to kill the

bitch act. I knew seeing my pretty ass face had her all up in her feelings anyway. I had no doubt that she knew that I used to be wifey. Clearly, she was intimidated, and that alone was enough. I was about to sprinkle a little dust of doubt and see how that worked for the two of them.

"Actually, you sure can leave him a message for me. Let him know that I stopped by and that he needs to call me so we can talk about the pregnancy." I gave my tight stomach a quick rub.

"Oh, and girl, don't let all that perfect man shit fool you. I was in the same position that you seem to be in. One minute I was working for him, the next minute I was fucking him. It's good for a while then the bullshit comes. The bitches, the lies, and for me ... a pregnancy that the nigga won't even acknowledge. But you don't gotta believe me, Alize. Just ask Melvina," I added, laying the lies on extra thick before walking out the door.

I couldn't help but laugh as I climbed back into my car and drove off. I had the silly bitch standing there looking stuck. Yeah, I'd lied, but that doubt was a motherfucker.

## ❧ 10 ❧

# MELVINA

I ain't even gon' front. I was big hating. When Alexis called and told me that Alize was fucking her millionaire ex-boyfriend, I felt a mixture of emotions. I wasn't sure whether or not to believe it. Alize didn't go after ballers. However, when Alexis said that she was all up in the nigga's business running shit, yeah, I was envious, but my chest was also swollen with pride. All that shit that happened to her in Vegas had changed her. I remembered telling her that I was going to show her better than I could tell her. Having Maine deactivate the keys and putting her ass out the room was all a lesson. Canceling her plane ticket home was a lesson. Calling my mama and telling her to charge her ass up, was a lesson. A very valuable lesson that had paid off for her. One that she fucking needed long ago.

Dealing with Neal had her blind. It had her feeling like everyone had her back and that just wasn't the case. My little cousin had to toughen up. Smarten up. And when she did all those things, I knew that she was going to boss the fuck up. My greatest irritation with Alize was that she thought she was better. Too good to do the shit we did. I saw the way she looked at me when I wore a lot of makeup. I saw the way her nose curled when she stared at my big ol' ass. She walked around like she was too good for all that shit, when bitches like me, were the ones that was getting the money. We were the ones that were winning. Alexis had the bag and fumbled it. She was a stupid bitch. She'd snagged a whole millionaire nigga and lost him. That shit baffled me. He was generous as fuck and let Alexis tell it, he was head over heels and sprung over her ass. I'd seen it with my own two eyes though. We'd met all them niggas around the same time and it didn't take long for Lance to fuck with her hard. Now she was coming to me talking about Alexis was stepping on her toes. 'Vina can you talk to her? Let her know I'm pregnant and that she needs to fall back while we work shit out.' Hell nah. At the end of the day, Alize was my family, and the nigga Lance wasn't fucking with her because of some shit that she did.

Alize had scored big, and I was going to see to it that I got back in her good graces so that I could snatch up one of his friends. Or ... maybe that crazy ass brother of his.

## 11

### NEAL

I couldn't lie, I felt like a sucker. Alize's ass had definitely played me, and it pissed me off even more because of who she'd played me with. That bitch had me thinking that she and I were going to get back together. That she was only working there to get paystubs so she could get an apartment. Had a nigga hopes up all high only to say fuck me.

That nigga Lance was the plugs plug. He literally supplied the nigga that supplied me. I didn't hold a torch to his ass, so I knew if Alize really fucked with dude, then there was no way that I was getting her back.

"You can't be mad at Alize for living her life," Boobie tried to reason with me while I rode shotgun in his heavily tinted, chalk-colored Mercedes Benz S550.

"Man, that bitch knew what she was going. She wanted a heavy hitter; she saw one and she went after him. How ironic was that shit, cuz? That bitch come into the shop snapping, see the nigga, then all of a sudden start working for him. I ain't buying that bullshit. Now they together."

I let out an angry sigh. I wanted my bitch back. Alize was a good woman for real. If Lance was a solid nigga, then he had a good bitch. Yeah, yeah, yeah. I knew what motherfuckers were thinking. Why would I cheat on her if she was a good woman? That's just the shit that niggas did, and now I was regretting it.

I still fucked Melissa from time to time, but it wasn't nothing serious. I had a few other hoes, but none of them compared to Alize. I knew I had wronged shawty. I should have done right by her. It was still fucked up that she left a nigga. The first time I was ever caught with my dick out and that bitch rolled. I wasn't about to be a big ass kid and say the shit wasn't fair out loud to Boobie, but it wasn't.

"Yo, can you swing me by the daycare to pick up the girls? I gotta pick up my car and feed them before I take them home. I gotta get there before my mama get there. She been buggin' about me leaving them at the daycare so late."

Boobie laughed. He knew exactly how my mama was when it came to her grandkids.

"Yeah, Aunt Judy be spazzing. You do need to stop leaving them there so late though. You just gotta stop moving at a certain time so you can get home earlier. Shut shit down at seven or eight. If niggas don't have what they need, then they don't fucking get it at all."

"Facts. That's exactly what I'm about to start doing. Alize go to court tomorrow though. I'm sure the judge will reinstate custody."

"You think so? Do she got everything in order?"

I turned and looked at that nigga like he was stupid. "Hell yeah. She fuck with that paid ass nigga too. Bitch just got a new crib out Buckhead. Driving around in a motherfucking Jaguar and shit."

Boobie laughed. "Who told you that? Aunt Judy?"

"Yeah, you know she always rubbing it in a nigga face that I fucked up a good thing. That I should have done right by her and all that bullshit. Now she telling me that if Alize happy, then I should let her be."

I shook my head just thinking about it. It was like a punch to the gut every time I thought about her with that nigga. The shit had me sick for real.

"She right though. Alize is cool as fuck. She does deserve to be happy. But you never know. That shit may not work, and you may get another chance."

A few minutes later, Boobie pulled his car into the small parking lot of the daycare.

"Don't be all day long nigga," he said, bringing his wrist to his face to check the time on his watch.

Despite what that nigga said, I took my time going inside. After scooping up my girl's belongings, they followed me outside and hopped in the car.

"Wassup y'all," Boobie greeted them from the front seat.

"Hi," they replied in unison.

"I don't know what y'all did, but they some good ass kids. I done fucked with some bitches that had some bad ass mother-fucking demonic kids."

"Put your seatbelts on," I told the girls before climbing back into the front and closing the door. I then turned to Boobie. "I don't know either. They never been really bad. They perfect for real," I said.

I looked back at my girls and flashed them a smile. The shit was kind of bitter-sweet. I really had a dope ass family and fucked it up. I used to cherish that shit when Alize and I first got together and started having babies. After losing my job and stepping out into the streets with Boobie, something just changed in me.

"You going back to your car right?" Boobie asked.

"Yeah."

Boobie shifted out of park and into drive and began heading back to his shop. Luckily, it wasn't far.

"So, what's up with the work situation?" I asked Boobie, while he drove.

"I'm 'bout to start fuckin' with this new nigga. I heard good shit about him."

"Yeah?" I looked to him and eyed him curiously. "So, you not fuckin' with Lance and his brother no more?" he asked.

"Na. After that little situation downtown, I spoke to Lance and he said he was out the game indefinitely. I ain't fuckin' with that nigga Lawrence if Lance isn't standing behind his product.

"Have you told him that yet?"

"Yeah. I hollered at the nigga earlier. Let him know that niggas was rocking with him after that bullshit he sold us."

"And what he say?"

"What could he say other than 'aight bet'. That nigga Lawrence ain't right for real. He sold niggas some bullshit that got the streets hot as fuck. Not to mention, everybody losing money. It was the nigga Lance who made shit halfway right by reimbursing everybody. Lawrence damn sure wasn't going to do it."

"Facts. And even still, a lot of niggas ain't gon' cop from us no more just because of that."

"Exactly. It's bad for business. And that nigga don't give a fuck because he up already."

"Right. But not for long."

"Why you say that?"

"Because the new nigga we 'bout to fuck with is 'bout to have shit on lock. Lawrence ain't gon' be able to get no money. At least not over here. Aye yo, why the fuck this nigga tail-gating me like this," Boobie stated abruptly, ending our conversation. I noticed the sense of urgency in his voice, so I leaned up a bit and peeked at the rearview mirror. Sure enough, there was a small, black Mercedes Benz traveling extremely close behind us.

"The fuck this nigga doing?" Boobie said. He had intentionally slowed down in the right lane. The left lane was open and whoever was driving didn't go around.

"Maybe it's an old person. Let them go around."

"That's what I was trying to get them to do," he said.

"Daddy, I'm hungry," Sage whined.

"Me too," Violet cosigned.

"Girls, I need y'all to sit back and be quiet, okay. Daddy's gonna make sure y'all eat," I assured them.

"Boobie, swing this corner and pull into the driveway of McDonalds."

I wasn't telling him to swing into the parking lot so I could get food. I wanted him to swing into the parking lot because I wanted to see if the motherfucker behind us was going to follow us.

Boobie did as told and made a right at the light. He then proceeded to pull into the McDonalds parking lot and head towards the drive-thru line. Before I could tell him not to do that bullshit, he pulled in and the lurking ass Mercedes pulled in right behind us. The way the drive-thru was set up, that move had us blocked the fuck in. Panic ripped through me when I saw the door of the Mercedes swing open and the driver hop out in all black. I pulled my gun off my waist.

"Boobie, grab ya shit! It's a hit! Girls get down!" I screamed.

I cocked my gun and spun back around to open fire through the closed window. I was too slow. The gunman's first shot was through the back window where my kids were seated.

All I could hear were their screams and frantic cries for help as the entire glass shattered down on them. The next thing that I knew, Boobie's connect, Lawrence was ripping the car apart from the Draco he was holding.

TO BE CONTINUED

Lightning Source UK Ltd.
Milton Keynes UK
UKHW011145100922
408645UK00001B/175